Pirates Come Down

Pirates Come Down

A Southern Ocean Saga

Christopher McMaster

Southern Skies Publications

ISBN: 978-1-99-117160-3 (paperback)

978-1-99-116011-9 (Epub)

www.southernskiespublications.com

Cover art: Vila Design at: www.viladesign.net

First Printing, 2022

For the 2021 cohort, brought together long enough to become friends, and then cast out on their own amongst the waves

The Fisheries Need You!

Do you like to work outside? Are you young and fit?

Help protect our resources, and make good pay.

Skimmers, Pulsers, Spotters and Ak-Aks needed.

Become a PAC-Man (or Woman) and defend our fish!

Adventure on the high seas awaits ...

Apply now at your nearest port!

1

Rickets danced in front of the weigh station, staying loose like a boxer in the ring, as the fillets dropped into the trays waiting below. He thought of this part of the factory as a video game, but with consequences. Get it wrong and there'd be hell to pay, the foreman biting his ear off or teammates helping him focus after the shift. Nothing like a team that starts to bitch. Or worse, docked pay. If he could spare any mental activity for computation, he would figure out how much each tray was earning the ship, the crew, and more importantly, himself. Seeing each tray as coin in his pocket would also help him stay focussed.

But he didn't dare take his eyes, or concentration, off the trays and the scales they sat on. When the scale read six point eight kilograms, he punched the black stopper, and even before the door of the chute closed and stopped the flow of fillets, he shifted the tray to the packing conveyor, put an empty tray on the scale, stuck on the right coloured tab—red, yellow, or black—and opened the door to let the backed-up fillets drop down.

When all three trays hit their limit at the same time—now that was fun. He cursed the foreman for setting the speed of the conveyor so fast. She expected everyone to run at one pace—hers. It was an impossible ask. She worked the trimming line, sorting each fillet by weight, cutting off any skin or bone missed by the machines. Her hands flashed as if they were possessed. But he'd try, his own hands moving, trays shifting, even doing a little footwork just to annoy Tarryn at her weigh station, making a game out of trying to get her to look over and lose her flow. She never did. Rickets glanced at the speed lever above him, tempted to move it to a slower setting, but he'd probably miss a tray.

It was a hell of a haul, at least forty tonnes. Skipper couldn't resist going for more if there was still quota left. It was a good season, the hoki were running, and there was money to be made. Lots of money. Enough to make Rickets try to keep up with the foreman, hands a blur, trays shifting. Hit the stopper, move the tray, replace the tray, fix on a coloured tab. Yellow, red or black, according to the size of the fillet. The pace meant time would fly, because the mind was occupied. Still, it was going to be an insufferably tiring shift processing this much fish, even with time on the wing. The deckies might come down and help after they tied the net down or set it for another haul, but Rickets would still be dancing in front of trays for hours. And the packers would be laying fillets into boxes, trying to keep up with him, trying to keep up with the foreman, trying to keep up with *Schlosen 221*.

The *Schlosen*. A marvel of butchering ingenuity that took a whole fish, cut off its head and tail, sliced it in half, disposed of its guts and shaved its flesh into the thin pieces of meat the world was hungering for. There were three of them occupying the factory, and all were purring as they sliced and diced. They still required a human to put the fish in the right way, to weed out the damaged carcasses, to sort out the by-catch, drive the ship, set the net. Deckies were still up top. And Rickets was still below. Maybe fishing hadn't changed that much, after all. It had just got a lot more efficient.

The scale with a tray on it marked with a red tab registered six point nine and he deftly hit the stopper, moved the tray, and placed an empty on the scale. As it began to refill, he heard the alarm. Four long blasts, followed by a pause, followed by four long blasts, and a pause, the pattern repeating again and again. Over the hum of machinery and blare of music, it still hurt his ears. It was meant to. That bell was for him. Rickets hit the stopper above the tray with a black label, moved the full tray to the packing line, replaced it with an empty. He tore off another black tab and stuck it to the new tray, his mind forcing his body not to leave the station, to wait until he was relieved. The golden rule, at least one of them out of a long list: never leave a station until relieved.

After what was probably a few seconds, but felt much longer, a hand touched his shoulder. He was half way to the sink and ripping off his gloves before his heart completed a beat. He watched his rubber apron fall on the deck after missing the hook, ran his hands under a stream of water, and bolted up the stairs leading out of the factory deck and into the changing room. Grabbing a PFD, he fastened it and stepped through the hatch leading to the trawl deck. The PFD was decoration, a tradition meant to make the wearer feel safe. If he was in the water, he was dead, period, and no personal floatation device was going to bring him back, because he was probably in several pieces. Rickets patted the toggle at the left side, the one to pull if he was somehow, miraculously, alive. That toggle activated the gas cylinder inside and filled the life vest with air. It helped a little, knowing it was there; reassuring in a pathetic way. At least something was on his side.

Rickets slowed his pace as he neared the speed boat. He passed the observer and slapped him on the shoulder, hard enough to make him stagger, hard enough to leave him wondering if it was encouragement or something else. To a lot of fishers, it was just the Government still looking over their shoulders. The observer's job was to monitor and report the catch, to watch while the crew harvested the nation's wealth. He counted the fish they hauled, watched as they worked, tested the size and sex of the fish, took biological samples to send back to the real scientists in Wellington. His data helped set the quotas, those mysterious numbers the fishers were given each year telling them how much they were allowed to catch and where.

"Watch this!" Rickets shouted as he passed.

The observer's work played a role in this somehow, Rickets figured. At least the government joined the team. But not just with observers, with real muscle. At the beginning of the century the New Zealand Navy had two frigates and a few patrol boats. Now it had about four times that, heavily armed and tasked with protecting the EEZ, known by fishers as the *Eazy*. The first E in that acronym was 'exclusive', meaning just that. Territorial waters that stretch two hundred nautical miles around the islands, for the sole use of Kiwis. While some countries had fished their stocks to oblivion, New Zealand managed theirs. The nation put a quota on target species, researched it, let the cowboys go out of business and sell their boats. At the same time, they continued to give the market what it wanted and to pocket the profit. As fish stocks died out elsewhere because other nations didn't bother with a quota management system, or couldn't enforce one, New Zealand's fish became more valuable. Only, as other fisheries played out, New Zealand waters started to look more attractive to other fleets. First, they encroached, shouting insults, cutting nets and ramming ships. Then they packed guns, which meant Kiwi fishers did too. Vessels were boarded, holds emptied. Fishers killed. By the time the Navy started acting like a navy, the fishing fleet already had PAC-Men and Droners on board.

Not that Rickets could see warships nearby right now. This fight was going to be theirs alone. As usual, he thought.

Manu, the spotter, was making himself fast to the bow. Rake grabbed her EMP pulser and sat behind him. Toby, the bosun, handed Rickets his skimmer as he climbed aboard, clipping on to the tether at his position. This was the bosun's boat, and as second mate he had something to prove. It meant he drove and drilled his crew, but that's why they were there, their primary role. Rickets was a PAC-Man. He didn't know where the name came from, some kind of old-school game or something, an old deckie told him. It didn't matter. Patrol and Attack Craft. That was the PAC part. He was the man. High risk, high pay, and as far from the factory as he could get. He was there to defend their fish, more than to gut or weigh them.

Rickets grabbed the side of the speed boat with his free hand as the crane lowered them over the side of the ship. Toby had the engine at full rev as soon as they hit the water. Rickets focussed on his skimmer as they shot over the surface, smashing through the waves. He opened the chamber and checked the missile inside was secure. It was a water line killer, punching a hole so large in the target vessel that nothing could stop the water. The missile flew so low it looked as if it skimmed across the surface to its target. Turning behind him, Rickets nodded to Anna, his loader, as she prepared the second missile. Two shadows flew quickly over them, the Droners going to work, sending out their deadly little pests.

"Identity!" Toby shouted over the din of the outboard and thump of the hull. "Who the hell is out there?"

Manu peered through his sighting lens, trying to keep level as the speed boat bounced over the swell. Two flashes off their starboard beam meant the Droners were doing their job, keeping the eyes of their mystery guest busy elsewhere. Both were hit, but others would follow.

"Identity!" Toby shouted again. His voice was getting shrill like it usually did when he was excited.

Rickets needed to know who it was too. If it was Chinese, he shot across the bow. A warning. A gentle way to tell them that they had strayed into the backyard, and would they kindly rectify what must have been an unwitting error of navigation and leave the exclusive economic zone. Sometimes his skimmer could be polite. There was some irony in that. Their insatiable appetite for fish depleted their own stock, as well as much of their neighbours, and gave New Zealand enough money to build the ships needed to protect their own from them. But politics was politics, so they'd play nice in order to not start a fight with their most important customer.

Now if it were Thai, Rickets aimed at that red line Lord Plimsoll invented over two centuries before to stop ship owners from overloading their vessels, turning them into 'coffin ships' as they sank to the bottom and brought their owners rich insurance pay-outs. The red line was the limit of the hull that could be submerged for the vessel to navigate safely. To Rickets, it made a wonderful target. He magnified his sights, searching for the line to send whatever fishers on board to the bottom of the sea in their coffin. They could have flown Kiwi flags like some of the foreign vessels contracted by New Zealand companies. They could have played by Kiwi rules, hosted the Kiwi observers, but they chose to steal instead. Conflict when the ships met was an unofficial agreement. They usually didn't meet because of that.

"Drone approaching, two o'clock!" Manu shouted.

"Rake—"

"I'm on it!" she barked at the bosun.

"Take it out!" Toby shouted at her.

"Wait ... for ... it ..." she growled.

The dark speck in the air grew larger as it tried to lock target on the attack boat. Rake moved her pulser to the right, and then to the left, to keep aim as Toby zigged and zagged. It was a race between its operator and their Pulser. After what seemed like minutes, but was probably just a second or two, she jerked back as she fired, an electro-magnetic pulse travelling at almost nine tenths the speed of light leaving her weapon and hitting the drone, killing all its power. Rake dropped the empty magazine and replaced it with the full charge her loader handed her as the dead drone fell into the sea.

"Identity!" the bosun shouted. Sounding like a little girl (no offence to little girls) Rickets thought behind his grin.

"Silhouette emerging," Manu said.

"That's not what I asked for!"

They should have detected the ship hours ago. It should never have gotten this close to their vessel, or their fishing grounds. There were rumours of radar reflecting paint. The ship floating out there must have been covered in it. Rickets didn't know who spotted her, but he promised to buy them a beer. If it was missed and night fell, they would have been boarded, their hold raided and their mutilated bodies tossed into the drink.

"I know this ship!" Manu shouted. "It's the *Bhangphu*! It has to be!"

They all knew that ship. The *Bhangphu*, a pirate Thai factory deep sea trawler, eighty-two meters in length with a crew of sixty-six. Sneaking into the *Eazy* to harvest fish before slinking back outside the zone and selling their catch. It didn't just take their fish, it took their future, it took their livelihoods. It was a tick sucking their blood, a leech, a vampire—whatever analogy made them the angriest. It was growing fat on their hard work and sacrifice. Those were close to the words the recruiter used, but Rickets didn't need to be sold. He understood the job, he even liked it. He tensed his shoulders, bracing a thigh against the side of the speed boat, the skimmer raised and steady and unmoving as the boat swerved and bounced.

"It's the *Bhangphu*!" Manu shouted again. "No doubt about it!" he added, but peered closer again at the ship.

Rickets didn't wait for further confirmation. He launched the missile, its exhaust plume streaking across the surface of the sea. Muscle memory took over as he opened the weapon and held the launcher at his side. Anna slapped a second missile in the chamber, which he closed and again aimed at the *Bhangphu*. He didn't have to fire it, but he did. A ball of fire filled his scope as the Thai vessel was torn open. He followed the second missile with his bare eye as Anna loaded a third into the weapon. Another explosion, closer to the bow, right where he wanted it. Toby slowed the boat and they all watched as the ship leaned onto its port, pointed bow down, and slid into the waves. They bobbed silently on the swell until the *Bhangphu's* stern disappeared beneath the waves.

Toby ended the moment by revving the outboard and turning the speed boat back towards their ship. Rickets shook his head. The bosun probably wanted to strut around the deck as soon as he could, while the crew all stowed their weapons and went back to the factory to continue processing the catch. He deserved it, but there was really no need to rush back for that. It was nice out in the fresh air, those fish in the factory weren't going anywhere, and there were plenty of other hands-on duty to finish them.

2

Stevens, the First Mate, stood on deck waiting when they returned to the ship. He was wearing that unreadable smirk that was neither smile nor frown. He squinted in the afternoon glare. He had the vampire shift—eight at night to eight in the morning. This was probably more sun than he'd seen the whole trip. It looked like he missed a shave or two, as well as laundry day, which was not unusual. But things were bad if he was awake at this time.

"You're wanted on the bridge," he said. "Both of you."

Rickets looked at Toby standing nearby, watching the bo-sun's mouth open and close. He would have had his brag rehearsed. His shoulders were already on their way back, his chest starting to puff. This was his moment, just what he'd been waiting for. Now he'd been pricked by a needle and Rickets smiled as he deflated. Rickets didn't care for officers, even those he liked.

"Now," Stevens added.

He turned, walked across the main deck and climbed the stairway. They followed. By the time they ascended the first flight, Stevens was already in the wheelhouse. Toby entered first and Rickets closed and made the door fast behind him. There were five in the room and it felt crowded despite all the space. Aside from the skipper, the observer was also there. Of course he was, Rickets thought. He had the right to be any place on the goddamn ship he wanted to be, and this was the place of interest at the moment. The *Aunty Cindy* just sunk a fishing vessel, and that didn't happen every day.

The observer approached Rickets with his hand out. He had heard his name before but was drawing a blank.

"Patrick," he said smiling, "it's good to see you back."

Nobody called him Patrick, not even his mother. Rickets glanced at the hand hanging in the space between them. The observer pulled it back when he figured it wasn't getting a date, and crossed his arms, copying Rickets' body language. Rickets knew that observers were taught that kind of thing. Being a sort of neutral on board, not crew, not company, just the nosey guest sleeping on the couch, observers often became a type of agony aunt or unofficial ship's councillor. Psychological First Aid, they called it.

The observer nodded, as if agreeing with something. "I'm always here if you want to talk," he said.

Amiable fucker, Rickets thought. The image of the observer's nose flattening against his face and blood spraying onto his chest as his fist smashed all the bone and cartilage sticking out of his skull filled Rickets' mind. He imagined his left coming in from the south and laying waste to an ear. The corner of Rickets' mouth twitched in an attempt at a smile, but he held it, and his hands, back.

"I'm fine," Rickets lied. With thoughts like those, he knew that he obviously wasn't.

"Rickets!" the skipper said. Van Loos had skippered the *Cindy* since she was commissioned. The PM Class fishers were built a decade ago, so he and ship were almost one being. Tall and lanky, he reminded everybody of an actor from old films they could never remember the name of. He walked over and thrust out a hand. Rickets took it and he squeezed firmly.

"Nice shooting. Damn fine shooting," Loos said. He let go of Rickets' hand and slapped his shoulder before returning to the chair in the centre of the room.

"And nice driving, Toby," he added. The bosun started to puff up again, getting ready to crow. "But now we have to sort some shit out." The words were like a punch to the poor man's chest.

"Who do you think you just sunk?" Loos asked. Rickets felt himself deflate a bit as well and stared with his mouth just as slightly open as Toby's.

"It was the *Bhangphu*," Toby said. "The *Bhangphu*. The same one that—"

"Are you absolutely certain?" Loos asked.

Toby swallowed. There was something in the word *absolutely*, or the word *certain*. Or how they both went together when the skipper said them.

"Manu spotted the silhouette, so yeah, totally certain." Toby didn't sound certain. "He was watching," Toby added, pointing at the observer. "He'd know."

"Are you certain it was the *Bhangphu* you shot at?" The question was for Rickets.

He swallowed. "No, sir," he answered. Rickets could feel Toby's eyes on him, but he kept his gaze locked on the skipper. "Manu called it, I just shot it."

"I can get him if you want," Toby said.

"Not now, bosun," Loos said. "I'm going to make a very important call, and need to clarify a few things before I get on the horn. We just sunk an unidentified fishing vessel and the admiralty is going to want to know why."

"Unidentified? Sir, it was the *Bhangphu*!" Toby said.

"The *Bhangphu* was spotted two days ago in the Central East fisheries zone," the observer said.

"Which means," Loos added, "Unless she can teleport, it wasn't the *Bhangphu* you sunk."

"Then who—"

"That's enough, bosun," Stevens cut in. "Moss told us what he saw, or thinks he saw," he said.

That was what the observer liked to be called, Rickets remembered, but it wasn't his real name.

"A lot of ships were built in the same ship yard, so it'd be easy to confuse it with all the others," Loos added. "Rickets, you had it in your scope, what did you see?"

"The ship was painted completely black," Rickets said. "Bow to stern. I took aim at the water line where I could see red. The hull still had some colour."

"Her hull was painted red?" Stevens asked.

"Yeah, water line down. There wasn't much showing, so she had to be pretty full. I timed it with the swell."

"Very low in the water," Stevens agreed. "I was lucky to see it on the radar."

Okay, Mr Stevens, Rickets almost said aloud, I owe you a drink.

"There's been talk of a paint that deflects radar," Moss, whose name was something else, added.

"It must have been dipped in the fucking stuff!" Toby was trying to be relevant in the discussion, but even though he was third in command it sounded like he was interrupting the adults in the room. They ignored him and went over to the radar.

They ignored Rickets too, and he didn't like it. "So, who did I kill?" he asked.

Stevens was pointing to a part of the screen. The observer was nodding. Skipper put his hands on his hips and leaned in.

Rickets raised his voice, not caring what he sounded like. "I asked, who the fuck did I just kill?"

They turned around and faced him, standing there quietly for the longest moment.

"Right now, we don't know," Loos finally said. "We do know that if you didn't hit it, it would have hit us. We lost a lot of drones intercepting her missiles, and didn't have many left. So, you did your job, and you did it well. That's enough to know for now."

Rickets disagreed. "You don't know who it was?"

"Not yet," Loos answered.

He walked over to the coffee maker and poured a mug. He came back and handed it to Rickets, who had to unclench his hands and unfold his arms to take it. He lifted it to his mouth, savouring the smell, then the taste. The observer could learn a thing or two from the skipper if he was serious about always being there to talk, Rickets thought.

"Admiralty has the feed from our attack, but they're drawing a blank," the skipper said. "And nobody has contacted them about a ship that has suddenly gone missing. They told me they've even asked the Chinese, for what it was worth, but got a firm denial. I can imagine their response, all offended that we'd think they might violate our *Eazy*." He went back to the coffee maker and poured himself a cup.

"Right now, nobody knows who was out there," he said after taking a swig. "Just that they were running ghost mode, deep in our waters, and stealing our fish. It's the paint admiralty asked me to confirm, which you three have just done."

He took another drink and nodded. "I imagine you want to clean your weapon, make sure it's free of salt water or whatever. Toby, how long until the shift is over?"

"Close to two hours," the bosun answered.

"It probably takes a couple hours to clean a skimmer," skipper said. "See that's done thoroughly. If there's one ghost around, there might be others."

"Yes, sir," Rickets said. He almost said thank you, but Rickets knew the skipper wasn't handing out a favour, he was dispensing charity. Rickets didn't know how to feel about that, if he should be insulted and refuse, take his place back at the weigh station or the gutting line. He didn't know how to feel about not knowing who he sunk. He took a long pull on his coffee, swallowed, and handed the cup to Loos.

"I'll get right on it," he said, leaving the bridge.

Rickets descended the iron stairs, crossed the deck and walked to the attack boat. The weapons locker was closed. Anna had no doubt already cleaned and stowed the skimmer. She was that kind of loader, just the type to have at your back. Rickets opened the locker and withdrew his cleaned and oiled weapon. Any trace of salt or residue powder was gone. He grabbed a rag and sat on the edge of the boat and began to rub the barrel.

He looked at the horizon behind the ship, the sea undulating into the distance. He knew he wouldn't see anything but water, that there would be no smoke or debris. They were trawling at close to five knots, so whoever it was he shot at would be kilometres away, and hundreds of metres deep. Rickets tried to feel as he did when pulling the trigger. The anger, the superiority, the rightness of being right there to do what had to be done. But he couldn't. His mind kept taking him under the water, into the cold depths. He wondered if he would go there in his dreams when he finally bunked, then opened the chamber of his skimmer and saw Anna had also cleaned and oiled there. He continued to wipe the already clean weapon.

Moss watched from the warmth of the wheelhouse, mug of coffee in hand. The deckhands stood beside the main deck as the cables retracted, water dripping onto the deck as the winches laboriously pulled the net back to the ship. He glanced at his watch, then at the GPS monitor and made notes in his worn notepad—time, date, latitude and longitude, and the end code, 2-C. He used endless code, all designed for the computers back on land. 2: 'End of tow determined by the observer.' C: 'When the net left the target depth.' Words would take too much space on the form, and all the code made sense to somebody. Moss had never met them, the data processors. He scribbled the sea bed depth, more data to be input later into the Catch Effort Log Book, the CELB, yet another code or acronym or initial. It was an independent record of every haul and every catch the vessel made.

He checked the coordinates again. They had steamed for ten hours and were over one hundred and sixty kilometres from the *Ghost Ship*, as it was now called on board. Or at least where the *Ghost Ship* once was. When that net was hauled, there wasn't a soul on the ship that wanted to stay and fish those waters. Moss flipped back through his notepad.

"Why'd you set the net here?" he asked.

"We've fished here before," Loos answered. "Figured it'd be worth a go." Unspoken words: it was closer to shore and safety.

There wasn't code for the real reason. Moss nodded at the code he had written earlier. C-1. C: 'Vessel apparently chose fishing location mainly because of reference to historical records'. 1: 'Skipper's decision'. One monitor on the bridge showed a mass of marks, lines clumped together in bright colours, each a record of previous trawls. Loos knew the grounds well, the fish in them and where they should be in any given season. The fancy technology only helped a little on top of the years of experience a skipper typically had.

"Looks like it may have paid," Moss said, pointing at a monitor. The bridge resembled a computer lab more than a wheelhouse on a fishing boat. Monitors formed a half circle around the captain's chair where Loos sat with his feet propped against the nearest counter. Three lights at the bottom of the screen indicated how full the net was.

"I think so."

"The lights seldom lie."

The question was, what was it going to be full of. They were after hoki. What they didn't want was what the factory hands called a grab bag, an assortment of different types of fish that each required their own manner of gutting and dressing—if they were worth keeping. If they weren't, the meal man would be kept especially busy. Moss made a point of visiting the meal men from time to time. There were only two, working separate twelve-hour shifts by themselves at the bow of the ship where the meal plant was located. Guts, heads, tails, worthless bycatch, all made their way on their own conveyor belt, got sliced and diced, then baked, until eventually they turned into powdery, dry meal that would end up as feed, either for other animals or for the earth as fertiliser. The meal men kept watch on the whole process, including stacking the forty-kilogram sacks filled with meal. It was lonely work, and Moss's visits were more a check on their well-being than on their product.

Loud clanging on the deck got Loos out of the chair and he walked to the stern-facing windows of the bridge. Moss followed, watching as the weights were dragged aboard. A few moments later the net surfaced, glistening silver.

"Looks clean," Moss said.

"Well, what's your estimate?"

"Hmm," Moss said. "Surface green weight ... twenty-four, twenty-five tonnes."

"A little fat on those numbers, don't you think?" Loos teased.

"Not at all, look at that thing, at least the part we can see!"

The deckhands moved with practiced efficiency, wrapping line around the net, connecting it to the yo-yo boom and signalling to the mate when it was ready. Loos operated the winch for the boom directly above the net and lifted it off the deck. Moving another control, he continued to bring the net towards the bow. More came on board as the net continued to be winched out of the water.

Moss whistled and jotted in his note pad. "Time to revise upward, I think."

"Still not agreeing," Loos said.

"Nobody says you have to," Moss said. "Twenty-eight tonnes. At least. Getting close to the quota, aren't you? The trip will be ending early if you keep hauling these."

"You're heavy again," Loos said. "No more than twenty-two. But you'll enter your number, not mine."

"You know it," Moss agreed. "I gotta trust my eye. Come on, look at that—another that size and you can head home with a full hold."

"It's not your eye I'm questioning, it's your guesstimate," Loos said, keeping to what had become somewhat of a script with the early morning hauls. "It'll equal out once all that's processed, and the numbers don't lie."

"That it probably will," Moss said, noting the time. With this size haul, processing would take hours, so he was in no rush to get to the factory. He pointed to a passageway above the deck. "I'll get my gear and take a perch over there."

"Enjoy the view," Loos said.

Moss softened his knees and let them bend with the rising and falling of the ship, keeping perfect balance. He kept his eyes on the horizon. A vivid orange brightened as the sun rose out of the water. Breathing in the cool morning air, he took the scene deep inside. He tried to catch as many sunrises as he could, a time out of time, not night and not day. They nourished him and made him forget, at least for that brief time, how far away from home he really was. As his own manager, he got to grab as many sunrises or sunsets as he wanted, but the timing of the haul this morning was perfect for doing his job as well as enjoying the view. As the deckies worked the net on the trawl deck, he crossed out his estimate and added a couple more tonnes.

Birds swarmed the waters around the stern of the boat, the constant companions at every haul. He checked the mitigation devices, a reflex at this point in the voyage. He'd seen them operating correctly every time. It would only be the exception that caught his eye. The bafflers still hung from the starboard and port of the vessel. It didn't take much to baffle a bird, simply hang a long line out from the ship with bright orange or pink pipe attached to the ends. Most birds care about their wings, and the coloured pipe swaying in the wind and swell is enough to dissuade most from coming too close or landing on the vessel. To prevent any clever chicks from sneaking through to help themselves to a meal, and probably get injured or killed in the process, the Battle Rope kept active. It was another case of fisher ingenuity, like the other mitigation devices the government adopted and mandated as required equipment. Simple and effective, a line draped with pink streamers was flicked outward along the side of the ship by a hydraulic arm. Moss hadn't bagged and tagged a single bird yet. He didn't mind that part of the job, and casualties sometimes occurred, but it saddened him to see such beautiful creatures with their wings mangled and torn, or soaked and drowned in a net. He made an estimate of the flock, noting species.

"So, this is what you get paid for? Bird watching?"

He didn't hear the footsteps behind him and flinched. He turned and saw Rickets standing beside him at the rail. "You scared me," Moss said.

"I sometimes have that effect. That's a mollymawk," Rickets said, pointing at dozens of the same type of bird swooping near the stern. "Oh, and there's another."

"They prefer the name Buller's Albatross, if you don't mind," Moss said in his best stuffy English accent. It wasn't very good. "They get quite upset if you call them anything else."

"My apologies," Rickets called overboard. It was lost in the wind. "I didn't know they were so fucking sensitive. Big baby birds."

"They're the smaller type of albatross," Moss added. "Those over there are the big ones."

"Looks the same to me," Rickets said.

"Look closer," Moss said. "The white between the wings means they're a greater albatross. And, come on, they're a lot bigger. Check out the head on the smaller ones. That one," Moss pointed at one swooping past. He made a jot in his small notebook, a number next to the species code for the bird, XPB. The 'X' denoted it as a bird, the 'B' and 'P' code for Buller's and Pacific albatross.

"That's the Buller's. See the greyish head? These others have white heads. They're called white caps," Moss said. "The Buller has a yellow bill with a bit of black."

Rickets leaned forward, staring at the birds.

"That big one sitting on the water is a Southern Royal." It was the longest conversation Moss had had with the PAC-Man since they left Lyttelton six weeks earlier, and the first words since those in the bridge after the sinking of the ghost ship. "Real big boy. Wing span wider than both your arms outstretched. More than you are tall. It's got the pinkish beak, but the tell is the black edge along its mandible."

Rickets nodded, looked at the bird, and then moved his gaze to the far horizon. Moss put his notepad in a pocket and faced him.

"Bird watching," Rickets repeated, shaking his head but smiling slightly.

"This looks like a lot of birds, but there used to be more," Moss said. "I do a count at least once a day, during a daylight haul."

"You're on deck early," he added after a moment. "Aren't you off shift?"

"Couldn't sleep," Rickets said without moving.

Moss waited, but nothing more came. He watched Rickets' jaw muscles work as the big man bit down on any other words. He could hear the deckies starting to empty the fish into the pound, the large stainless steel holding tanks in the factory below. He should get down there soon, watching and recording, refining his estimate. He dug in his pocket for a pack of gum instead and offered it to Rickets. Rickets took a piece, stuffed the gum into his mouth and the wrapper into his jacket pocket.

"Couldn't fall asleep, or dreams waking you up?" Moss had had the impression that the man was about to punch him when he first greeted him on the bridge. Rickets looked different now, not smaller, but less threatening, almost vulnerable, as if a layer had been removed by whatever plagued his mind.

"Dreams, yeah, if you can call them that," the man said. "Like drowning in black syrup. Like the air has been sucked out of—" Rickets stopped talking as quickly as he began.

"It doesn't matter who that ship was," Moss said. "It was us or them. And you saved us. So, thank you."

Rickets turned back to the birds following the boat, their wide wings riding the breeze towards the bow, effortlessly dipping one towards the water and almost touching the surface as they banked and flew in another direction. Others would drop their feet like landing gear, flap once or twice and land, riding a wave as the boat moved past.

"I'm serious," Moss said. "I wasn't fully aware of the danger we were in when I signed on. I'm scared shitless now. Honest. I'm glad you're on board."

Rickets made a sound that could have been a laugh.

As if on cue, three drones left the ship, the quiet hiss of their propellors quickly disappearing with the craft. Moss had noticed a lot more activity recently, tried to lighten the meaning by thinking up a species code for them.

Rickets watched until the drones were out of site, turned, and slapped Moss on the arm. "Better hit the sack," he said and walked away.

Moss stood watching as he opened the hatch to the companion way and latched the door. He glanced at the bridge as a voice piped over the loudspeaker, Loos barking at the deckies.

"Let's turn and burn, guys. Set the goddammed net! Last haul. The sooner it's full the sooner we're home," he said.

Moss left the deck through the same hatch Rickets used, but rather than head to a cabin he went to the locker room. He put on coveralls, hair net and steel-toed gumboots, and opened the door to the factory. A wave of sound hit him, dimmed only slightly by his ear muffs. He descended the steps to the factory below. Eyes left their work station and darted towards him as he stepped onto the decking, hands no doubt curious about the size of the haul, and the amount of work they faced. Machinery still hummed, but noise seemed to cease when he entered, as in a badly acted movie. He held up three fingers, then made a zero. Thirty tonnes. A few shook their heads. A moment later the factory hands were focussed on their tasks.

Water sloshed beneath the grating where he walked. Moss put on gloves and made his way to the pound where the fish from the recent haul were held. He tried to make eye contact with factory workers as he passed, smile or nod a greeting, but only a few met his gaze, and those seemed distracted, preoccupied. Scared, Moss admitted, just like himself.

He made his way to the stern to assess the fish and the size of the haul. It was a clean bag, over eighty percent hoki, and big ones at that. He noted the different quota species mixed in with them, took notes of their code and an estimated amount. LIN, 500. Ling made Moss think of dinosaurs. Everything about them seemed primordial. Eel-like bodies, mottled pink camouflaged flesh, bony narrow heads and rows of sharp teeth, they swam and they ate, unless something bigger ate them or scooped them out of the water in a huge net. And there seemed to be about five hundred kilograms of them. It was guesswork, but with practice he was becoming more and more accurate.

He considered another species. HAK, 400. Hake was more like a proper fish, Moss thought, at least they had fins and scales. He carefully lifted a spiny dog by the tail, set it back down on the conveyor. There were quite a few of them, so he wrote SPD, 800. The little sharks were well defended, with teeth in the front and a nasty spike that could go through a boot at the back. They seemed to be in every catch, including this one. He looked at a fish similar to hake, except with larger eyes and a cooler name, 'ribaldo'. He jotted, RIB, 300.

After a few more notes he selected one of the species for mid-level biological work, collecting data for the scientists in Wellington or wherever they studied. Grabbing a container, he pulled twenty ribaldo from the conveyor and tossed them in. He took the sample to his work station, weighed the fish, made a note on his tablet, and took the first one out. He measured it, sliced it open and noted the stage of the ovaries, then shaved the top of its head off. Using tweezers, he probed inside the brain cavity and withdrew the otoliths, ear bones that were used to tell the age of the fish ('just like the rings of a tree' a visiting scientist explained to him in training) and probably a lot more that Moss didn't know about. He was just the eyes and hands for those in the laboratories. But data was data, and it was what they asked for—numbers and samples.

He heard the clank of the net above him and smiled, hoping that Loos meant what he said, last haul and home.

4

Land never looked so good as Moss gazed from the bridge's wide windows. The appearance of green always brought a smile, as well as the thought of a proper cup of coffee. And then, after a debrief in Wellington, Mel and their little flat in Nelson. Weeks away were manageable, as long as he knew he was returning. This time he realised that wasn't always a certainty. Land looked good because he wanted to get off the ship and keep walking, all the way to that little flat if that's what it took.

Rickets was in the PAC boat, moving what appeared to be weapons and securing them in a steel locker beside the craft. The spotter, Manu, carefully carried a wooden box, waiting for Rickets to finish. As soon as the bigger man left the locker, Manu slid the box in. He turned from the locker and stared at the approaching harbour for a long moment before returning to his work. Moss recognised that look because he wore the same. Get off, walk away. Just keep going. Every fibre in his body yearned for it. He was sure Manu, Rickets, and the woman who sat behind Rickets in the boat felt the same way. But they would all sail again, and they all knew it, including himself. Mel was going to be pissed.

Rickets caught Moss staring. He raised a hand holding an invisible pint glass and took a big drink, then raised a thumb. Moss put his hands out. A shrug. He shook his head and frowned. Rickets knew the rules. Observers were neutral, the face of the Ministry, professional in dress and behaviour. There was nothing Moss wanted more than to join the shore party and drink his share of pints, and after the last email from the observer office in Wellington, he was in a mind to shove the rules up their dark place and get good and drunk.

Loos looked over a crew manifesto on the bridge as the pilot guided the eighty-metre vessel to its assigned berth. He put a light mark next to those he knew would return to ship. Some of them had nowhere else to go. Some were in it for the career, long timers like his engineers and factory supervisors. He put a circle next to other names. The circle was a question mark, but nobody glancing at the list would know that. Some new kids in the factory, a couple of deckhands. Loos watched Stevens from the corner of his eye. The mate was arranging watch for while they were in port. Stevens put his name on tonight's, letting others have a night on the town while he babysat the ship. Loos made a mark next to his name.

The company could replace the others, any who slipped away. They would pull from their applicant pool and fill any gaps. As for the others, any wavering, Lyttelton was a small port, which had distinct advantages. Small ports had less area to monitor and secure. There was only one entrance to the vessels, and only one exit. Easier to watch and lock down.

The colourful wooden houses lining the hills were for residents. Lyttelton was a bedroom community for the larger city of Christchurch. It was for working folk, not clubs and brothels. Those were through the tunnel and kilometres away in the city. Transport would be needed to reach those, and the company made sure that wasn't going to be available. Loos hated the precautions, but he needed crew, as did their sister ship, the *H. Clark*, berthed nearby. They both needed skilled hands to return to sea, which was the plan. The ships rarely spent more than a few days in port before re-supplying and going back to work.

There was only one pub large enough, and stocked well enough, for his crew, and that was where he would shepherd them. They could get as drunk as they wanted, and the van would be waiting to take them back. Or they could walk. It wasn't far, because Lyttelton was a small port.

"Don't get so wasted you won't be able to work tomorrow," he told the crew standing on the forecastle deck with him. He would have called them together in a muster drill, but wanted to avoid any use of alarms unless they were absolutely required. One of those was enough on this trip. They weren't necessary in Lyttleton. He called those on deck up with a shout and a wave of his arm, and Stevens rapped on cabin doors to summon any off duty.

"I don't want to find anybody sleeping on the gang plank in the morning, either." Loos didn't look at the factory manager, but several others did. At sea the man was one of the most professional and hardworking members of his crew. On land it was different.

"He made it to the second step, somehow," Rickets murmured to Moss, who tried not to look towards the manager, and shook his head in disbelief. "Join us, you need it," Rickets added.

"You know the rules," Moss said.

"The port's providing a van to get us all back home," Loos said louder, glancing at the two men. Both closed their mouths. "Sign out at the wheelhouse when you leave the ship, wear a high-vis vest until you leave the port gate, and sign back in when you're back on board. Stevens is on watch, and he'll be watching. And no bartering watch responsibilities," Loos added. "No one is to sell their watch. I don't care how bad you want to go ashore tonight. You're rostered on watch tonight for a reason, and you'll get your time ashore."

"You can get hundreds if you take someone's watch off them," Rickets whispered. "Especially the first night."

"This is a quick turnaround," Loos continued. "Empty the holds, re-supply, and a bit of a refit. Van leaves for the pub at eight, at the end of shift, so I'll see you then."

Loos ended the meeting by walking back into the wheel-house. Rickets slapped Moss on the back before returning to the PAC. "Come to the pub. You'll enjoy it," he said. "Rules are to be fucked."

Moss answered with another smile and shake of his head. He waited for the man to descend to the deck before col-lecting a high-vis from the wheelhouse and signing out. The crane was lifting pallets filled with boxes of frozen fish from the hold, over the railing of the ship, and placing them on the dock in front of a waiting forklift. Once the load cleared the gangway, Moss waved to the bosun operating it. He nodded in reply, and Moss stepped down and off the ship. He walked across the port to the small security office, waited until the guard checked his name on a list, took off his vest and dropped it into a waiting box, and picked up his pace.

After the chain link fence the road bent sharply up to the main road. Moss felt his leg muscles start to burn after the first stretch, and he started to pant. Each trip took its toll on fitness, at least in certain parts of his body. Like leg muscles and lungs. At the top of the hill, he texted ahead. Seven words, which should be enough. Pepperoni and olive. See you in ten. If he walked slowly, which he planned to do, the pizza might be ready as soon as he arrived. Fresh out of the oven. He paused and used the view to look over the ships in port. The *Aunty Cindy*, home away from home for the past six weeks. Nobody called her by her proper name, the *J. Ardern*. Sometimes just *Aunty*, or maybe just *Cindy*. Moored next to her was another of the new PM Class trawlers, the *H. Clark*, known better as *Helen*. Every company themed the names of a new fleet. For some reason the owner was into past leaders. They were comfortable boats, and great postings, until ghost ships started shooting at them.

Tomas, the observer from *Helen*, should have gotten the text and be ordering the pizza now. He picked a good time to step off of *Helen*. From the spark of welding torches and movement of cranes, a lot of work was happening there. Observers have little to do except get in the way during shore work. Moss saw the longer Russian ship, *Andropov*, in her mooring. Lyttelton was her home port. She was one of the ten foreign owned vessels operating in the *Eazy*, contracted by a New Zealand company, flying the New Zealand flag and operating under New Zealand laws. Many of the fishers on board, no doubt, also had New Zealand girlfriends in town. Moss observed on her before and liked them. The décor was an example of post-Soviet retro, with a touch of oligarch excess in its gilded cabin accessories, but she fished well and served good food. Docked beside her were a pair of navy corvettes.

Moss scratched the back of his neck and walked away, preferring not to think about why they were there. He looked at the wooden houses lining the hills around the port instead, imagining what they might look like inside, if they had wooden floorboards or open fires in the lounge. Part of being away from his own home and girlfriend for weeks or months at a time was the pay cheque at the end of it, each one closer to a down payment to buy into their own Kiwi Build. Getting on the First Time Buyer list might be a lottery, literally, but having the starter money wasn't. That was just down to hard work, meaning months at sea for him.

Tomas sat at a table, with a large pizza in front of him, when Moss walked into the restaurant. Moss breathed in the aroma of cheese and pepperoni.

"Man, that smells good!" he said.

Tomas stood up and hugged the taller man.

"I need this every time," Moss said.

"I'm still trying to make the land stop moving up and down," Tomas said.

Moss sat at the table and peeled a piece from the pie. "Never felt that," Moss said. "As soon as I step off, the ground is as solid as it should be. If you're too land sick, I could manage this by myself." He put the piece slowly into his mouth, closed his eyes and bit.

"Now that's what I'm talking about!" he said after swallowing. He smiled at his friend. "Get your email?"

Tomas took a piece of pizza. "Yeah, I got my email." They both ate in silence until ready to start their second slice. "They can't make us go out again," Tomas said.

"Yeah, they can," Moss said. "Especially if you want to keep this gig. The board must be empty. My supervisor sounded apologetic."

"Your FOS is Sandy?"

"She's sweet," Moss said. He met his fisheries observer supervisor at his pre-trip briefing in Wellington. She looked fresh out of high school, and small enough to lift with one hand. But she had a degree in marine science and worked as an observer herself for several trips. She knew what it was like to be an observer, and she, like the other FOS, knew what they were asking of him. "But I've been handed to Aden. He means well."

"Means well? Your ship was attacked. I wouldn't blame you if you just went home."

"It's not their fault, they're just doing what they're told," Moss said. "And I need the money. Like almost everybody else on these boats. There aren't too many jobs that pay as well. What are you still doing here?"

"What I'm told, that's what," Tomas said. "And trying to make mortgage payments. An empty jobs board is making the FOS's desperate, and just like you, I need the money. Besides, *Helen*'s a good ship."

"What are they doing to her?" Moss asked. "Looks like she was growing little appendages."

"Same thing *Aunty Cindy* is going to grow, state of the art thermal imaging radar, and a few more drone launchers." Tomas finished another piece of pizza. "Did you see the corvettes?"

"All two of them," Moss said.

"They're going to escort and patrol when we go out. You, us, and the Russians."

"One rogue ship, and we're forming convoys to go fishing now?" Moss asked.

"Yeah," Tomas said. "One is already too many. And I don't think they're telling us everything."

"Meaning?"

"I don't know," Tomas said. "The priority is to keep the fishing going, and make quota. The companies have to make their money, after all. Nothing else matters. The Ministry seems to agree."

"Fuck 'em," Moss said.

"Hey. At least they're buying us pizza," Tomas said. "Can't complain about the meal allowance."

"You know what I want to do?"

"Go on."

"I want to go the pub with the crew and get smashed," Moss said.

"You know the rules," Tomas said, sitting up stiffly. "We are independent, not part of the crew. Can't be seen to be partial. Can't be off drinking with them. Face of the government and all that."

"Was that a British accent?" Moss asked. "There is no independent. We all got shot at. And a wise man told me not so long ago, 'rules are meant to be fucked'."

Moss knew the pub; it was the only one in town. A favourite spot with students from the University of Canterbury, it was usually full to overflowing. Tonight was no different. Trendy twenty-somethings, and younger, crowded the bar, lining up five deep to buy drinks. The guys were dressed in a style Moss could only describe as Southern Man – plaid shirts, denim jeans and hairy faces. Beards were back in vogue. The girls all seemed as beautiful as flowers to Moss, even more welcome a sight than green hills. He smiled, thinking of Mel in Nelson, then sighed thinking about how long it might be until he saw her again.

Loud laughter brought him back to the crowded pub. He looked at a corner booth and saw Rickets crowded at the table with other crew from *Cindy*. Rickets climbed out as soon as he saw Moss. Weaving his way through uni students he grabbed Moss in a bear hug, slapping his back.

"I knew you'd make it," he said, releasing the observer.

"Just fucking some rules," Moss said.

"As you should!"

"This is Tomas," Moss said, almost shouting to be heard. "Observing on *Helen*."

"Argh, another one," Rickets said. "What are you drinking? Probably one of those twenty-dollar beers, right?"

"Don't I deserve it?" Moss asked.

"Nobody deserves a fucking twenty-dollar handle!" Rickets said. "Manu's at the bar with the money. Manu!" he shouted.

Manu slowly turned around at his name. Rickets looked at Moss.

"Indian Pale Ale," Moss said.

"Two," Tomas added.

"Fucking figures," Rickets said. "Two 'girly' beers!" he shouted at Manu.

"You better go help him," Rickets said. "He's trippin' on acid right now."

"Where'd he get that?" Moss asked.

"Me," Rickets said.

"You gave him acid?"

"He asked me," Rickets said. "Now go get the drinks. And make sure he comes back with six rum and Cokes. And whatever he wants."

Rickets made his way back to the table as Moss and Tomas struggled to reach the bar. Manu stood in front of the bartender, staring above his shoulder. Moss put his hand on his arm. "You okay, Manu?" he asked.

"What's that?" Manu asked.

Moss followed Manu's gaze. "That's a doll with lipstick all over her face hanging by her foot," he said. "And wearing a little bra made out of walnut shells."

"He's gonna have a lot to trip on in this place," Tomas said. Goldfish bowls hung suspended from the rafters with surreal dioramic scenes played out in them, and posters from another century that glowed fluorescent decorated the walls.

"Faaaw," Manu managed to say.

"Did you order?" Moss asked.

"Faaaw," Manu said again, studying the doll. "That just ain't right."

"Six rum and Cokes, and two pints of IPA," Moss told the bartender. He looked at Manu. "And a ginger beer," he added.

"You got the money?" he asked Manu.

"Oh man," Manu answered, shifting his gaze to the rafters and the little worlds suspended there.

Turning Manu towards the fishers' booth he gave him a gentle push. Manu started to walk in that direction. Moss reached in to his wallet and took out two hundred dollar bills. He waited a moment for change before realising there was none. He and Tomas carried the drinks to the table, and everybody squeezed closer together to fit them in. Moss swallowed a mouthful of beer and wiped his mouth with the back of his hand.

"Don't try to keep up with these guys," he warned Tomas.

"I thought you wanted to get drunk?" Tomas said.

"Yeah, but I want to at least remember where I was!" Moss replied.

He set his pint glass on the table at the same time as a full one was placed next to it by the bosun, Toby. He spread glasses out from a tray, more rum and Cokes, a cider, a drink Moss couldn't name. Toby squeezed in beside them.

"You gotta listen to this," he said, pointing with his thumb at the booth directly behind them. Moss and Tomas leaned back to listen to the conversation. They recognised the voice of Loos.

"Why's he talking that way?" Moss asked.

"He always does it," Toby said.

"Talks in a bad Russian accent?"

"Whoever he's talking to, he takes on their accent," Toby said. "He probably doesn't know he's doing it."

They turned back to their own table. Manu stared intently at the bubbles in his drink. Rickets handed the woman that sat across from him on his PAC a pill similar to one he held in his own hand and they put them in their mouths and swallowed. More full glasses arrived, crowding the table and only keeping up with the empties because the bus boy kept clearing them. At the end of each pint Moss looked around the table and saw different faces, as crew left and others took their seats. Moss tried to remember how many pints he had drunk but gave up. He put an arm around Tomas, picked up his beer and made a toast only he could hear.

"Fuck it," he said, and drained his glass. "Who needs to remember?"

5

The *Cindy* sailed on Sunday evening, three days after docking. Stevedores worked around the clock to unload cargo and load new supplies. Technicians affixed and tested new technology. Hungover crew formed chains and moved stores throughout the ship, where there was a place for everything and everything was put in its place. By the time they steamed, most of the substances that shouldn't be in their bodies had sweated out. Stevens took the helm, allowing those that needed rest to get it. The fishing grounds were over eighteen hours away. A lot of work still needed completing before then, but there was enough time to enforce a break. He followed the pilot boat away from the mooring. A corvette was already at the entrance. *Helen*, the *Andropov* and the second corvette would soon follow.

Within an hour the ship took on the familiar movements of the open sea, favouring the starboard side and rising and falling in the southern swell. Moss made an instant coffee and sat at a galley table. Shifts were resuming and crew finished their breakfast before heading to the factory. At this point in a trip there wasn't much for an observer to observe. He watched some of the new faces. Several crew had managed to miss the sailing, most of them trainee factory hands with the lowest pay and fewest benefits, not yet aware of all the perks coming with hard work in the fisheries. Like consecutive trip bonuses, as well as additions to the pay cheque as part of the percentage of the catch. It takes more than one trip to climb up that ladder, and those jumping ship barely touched the first rung.

Moss looked at the green faces at the table and smiled. "It'll pass," he said. "You just need to throw it up and get it out."

One of the new crew got up quickly and made his way down the companionway, swaying with the movement of the ship.

"It's your body getting used to the movement," he added for the two remaining.

He took a drink of coffee and gazed out the window. It wasn't a particularly smooth sea for their first trip, if it was their first. After being on land for a few weeks, Moss went through the same thing. Feel about seventy percent, start to burp a lot, then pray to the porcelain god. By the second day all was well, and constant movement was the accepted norm. He'd heard from others who it affected differently, even depending on what ship they were on. One observer knew a specific vessel as the 'diet boat.' She was fine on any other ship, but for some reason, when she was on that one, she felt sick almost all the time and hardly ate for weeks, or hardly kept down what she managed to eat. Aside from a brief adjustment period, Moss never had an issue. He examined himself, trying to feel his gut and his inner balance. Everything seemed fine, like he had never stepped off the boat. So far.

The new crew got up and made their way to a companionway and towards the factory. All the conveyor belts that were taken off and cleaned after the last trip now had to be reassembled. Take it apart, clean it, put it back together again. That's how fishing ends and that's how fishing starts, at least in the factory. Moss wondered how their first day would go, confined below deck, with no windows, crawling around and on machinery as their world moved up and down. He took another drink of coffee and smiled, happy it wasn't where he would spend his day.

On the second day out, Loos wanted to test the gear. He adjusted the pitch of the propellors, and the lift and pull of the boat surging through swell decreased with the speed. The eighteen-knot cruising speed became a leisurely four and a half. After rushing past, the ocean now seemed to grip the ship. Thompson Hole was a favourite of Loos', always good for a few full bags of hoki. Any deep depression a captain found was named after him. Loos didn't know who Thompson was, nor gave him much thought. The days of finding any new geographical features on the bottom of the ocean were long past. But five hundred metres down on the edge of the hole, the hoki liked to swim. Their prime target was the squid beds in the subantarctic fishery, but each captain was issued a shopping list from the company, orders to fill and orders of priority. Hoki was always wanted, so if he had a chance to stock up, he would take it. He didn't care to share the spot with the *Helen* or the *Andropov*, and the marks would now be plotted in their records if they weren't already on them, but he grudgingly admitted that there was enough to go around. Their factory hands and PACs needed warming up, just like his.

"Deck crew, get ready to set," he said into the mic on the bridge.

Deckhands emerged from their locker room and started prepping the gear. Net was stretched down the central trawl deck, untwisted and laid flat. The end barrier of the ship was lowered and the net slid off the stern. Bobbins clanked down the deck, the heavy weights clacking noisily until sliding into the water. Lines of large yellow and blue floats followed. When nothing but chain remained, the deckies attached the heavy trawl doors and the central runner. The bosun gave a crisp hand signal to the bridge, and the nets were lowered from the stern of the vessel to disappear below.

Loos monitored the doors as they descended and spread apart in the deep, opening the mouth of the net. He programmed seventeen hundred metres of warp to play out, allowing the net to reach the bottom five hundred metres below and trail far behind the ship. Taking his seat in front of the monitors, he watched the colours, blue for the cold water and orange and red for the warmer seabed.

"Come on, fishies," he said to the screen, waiting for oranges and reds above the seabed to fill his net. On the bridge of *Helen*, and on the *Andropov* fifteen kilometres behind, the captains were probably doing and saying the same.

Toby joined his team at the small craft. It was new, like most of their equipment, brought aboard at Lyttleton. PFD's with water activated gas cylinders, inflating the vest when submerged. Personal locating beacons, which sent a signal to orbiting satellites. Lights, bells and whistles. Even the weapons had been upgraded. The voyage to the fishing grounds would give them time to train with them, which was not enough in Toby's opinion. Everything felt rushed. He ran his eyes over his crew, checking their gear was on and secured properly over their new naval survival suits. They looked sharp. It wasn't just the suits. Of the two PAC's on board, he knew he had the better crew. Tisha, the other PAC skipper, might think the same about hers, but she would be wrong. They were the PAC that had sunk the ghost.

Manu attached himself to the bow, readying his spotting equipment. Rake and her loader checked the EMP charges on all their rounds. Rickets and Anna did the same. Toby read the display on the outboard, oil, fuel, air flow. Everything was new, so the drill was welcomed. Their new SOP's, standard operating procedures, for every trawl: both PAC's were to lower with the nets and fan out for the duration of the trawl, covering visually what the radar might miss. No more factory duties, and definitely not waiting to be tapped out before defending the ship. Extra crew were taken on to work the factory while the PAC-Men maintained a watch. It meant no more fish gutting, sorting lines or weigh stations. But it also meant hours of cold and wet in a speedboat with no shelter from either.

A storage box between their benches held smoko—flasks of hot coffee and, Toby hoped, plenty of hot food—so this would also be the cook's first test. Toby was briefed on the drill, and despite being tempted to give his crew a heads up, he did as he was told for the moment and left them in the dark. Knowing what's coming might make them look good, but looks don't save lives. Those were Loos' exact words, seemingly reading both the PAC skippers' minds. Do not tell your crews what might come at them. Disarmed attack drones controlled by Droners just as intent on looking good, coordinates for non-existent targets for skimmers to hit, each missile programmed to self-destruct at two kilometres distance. That is, *if* the captain and First Mate told him what was actually going to be thrown at them.

As the PAC hit the water, Toby accelerated away from the *Cindy*.

"They're gonna throw drones at us," he shouted forward. "Expect a couple simultaneous. And there'll be skimmer co-ordinates."

Rake turned and gave him a nod while Rickets held up a thumb. He took the PAC eight kilometres away from the *Cindy* at sixty degrees off the course of the trawler, then increased the distance as he moved them forward, until they were twelve kilometres distant, and the ship was no longer visible. The sea looked large enough to swallow them; they were a tiny speck on the massive undulating surface. Manu scanned from left to right with high powered binoculars built into a helmet. He acted like a kid at Christmas when they were issued, as if they were actually given to him personally. More bells and whistles, but more effective for spotting. Military grade.

Toby's eyes shifted from his spotter to Rickets' loader. He liked having Anna close. Her fine blonde hair whipped in the wind. She liked it when he ran his fingers through it and massaged her scalp—but only in their cabin. She was firm about no PDA's on deck. Public displays of affection. What a stupid acronym, Toby thought. There were enough acronyms on a ship without having to include handholding. She was right though, and it would have been totally inappropriate, but it was sometimes very hard not to reach out and touch her. His eyes travelled down her back to her thin hips. He smiled.

"Here come the little fuckers," Manu called, snapping Toby back.

"Initiating zig-zag pattern," Toby said, veering the PAC to port.

"And a target, no, two! Bearing zero six five true and zero nine eight true!" Manu called.

"Keep your head down, Rake," Rickets ordered, rotating his weapon with the movement of the PAC.

"Keep your own fucking head down, Rickets," Rake retorted. "Three simultaneous. Looks like more behind. Confirm, Manu." She activated the charge on her pulser.

"Too much interference," Manu called.

"Lining them up," Toby shouted, his voice edging higher. He took a breath, fighting the adrenalin. Anna teased him about his voice when he got excited, and he was sure the rest of the crew did as well behind his back. "You're on your own Rickets, take out your targets."

He didn't hear what Rickets replied, as he increased acceleration and turned the PAC in a wide arc. Droners usually thought in straight lines, so he'd help them out, forcing them to get behind each other.

"Head!" he heard Rickets shout.

Anna leaned to the side and Toby found himself staring down the barrel of Rickets launcher. He leaned over and felt the exhaust from the skimmer warm the side of his face. Rickets lowered the launcher and Anna slammed another missile into the waiting chamber. Toby sat up and glanced back, trying to see where Rickets' shot went.

Rickets was counting. "And one, and two, and three, and ..." An explosion followed. "Your goddammed head!" he shouted.

Toby leaned the other way and felt the heat of another skimmer pass by.

"Straighten the fucking boat!" Rake yelled. "Yeah, come on bitches, come and get it!" She fired a pulse, ejected the casing and held her rifle back. Lockey, her loader, inserted another EMP, and she took aim again. Toby ignored the explosion of the second skimmer and followed Rake's eyes to watch three drones lose momentum and dive into the sea five hundred metres away.

"Incoming!" Manu shouted. "Two drones, wide angle, two seven zero and one eight five."

"Fuckers!" Rake growled. "Distance?"

"Two kilometres. Each."

"Fuckers!" Rake repeated.

Toby steered the PAC due west, directly at one of the drones. He could hand her one of them, but there was no way to line them up.

"Grab the ak-ak, Manu," he called forward. "Give that son of a bitch to the south something to fly through."

Manu shouldered the fat barrelled rifle that was secured near his feet. It looked like an ancient blunderbuss and accomplished much the same thing—spray out fragments in the drone's flight path. Ancient anti-aircraft technology, adapted for another century.

"Mind your ears," the younger man said, and started firing off rounds. A hollow whoomph followed with a deafening boom.

On the other side of the PAC, Rake took aim. "Come and get it," she said slowly. Manu fired another pattern of four rounds and Rake fired the EMP. Lockey had a fresh EMP ready as soon as the used was discharged, but it wasn't needed. The drone to the south disintegrated as it flew through shrapnel and the other simply dropped into the sea. Manu stowed his ak-ak and scanned the skies. The crew waited, tense, ready.

"Skies are clear," Manu said.

Shoulders relaxed and weapons started to lower.

"About lunch time," Toby said, trying to deepen his voice and sound calm. "Manu, hand me your new glasses. I'll watch while you guys eat. Save me something." He caught Anna's eye and winked. He glanced at his watch. Another four hours, enough time to haul, set again, and come in with the second net. They didn't mention any more practice attacks, but that didn't mean one wouldn't come. Toby programmed a course into the outboard, and put on the spotter's gear. He listened to his crew celebrate their victory as he scanned the empty horizon.

The PAC was lifted aboard the *Cindy* the same time the net of the second haul was winched onto the trawl deck. Rickets stepped off with his skimmer and looked up at the windows to the bridge where Loos and Moss stood. Loos was working the cranes that lifted the large net while Moss just watched. Paid to watch birds, paid to watch others work. Some guys had all the luck, Rickets thought. He noticed Moss looking his way and nodded to him. He took his cleaning gear from the locker, sat on a round of cable and started rubbing salt water off each surface. It was all reinforced polymer, not susceptible to rust or corrosion, but if he took care of the weapon, he figured it would take care of him. He cleaned and oiled the barrels. He didn't have to think about what he was doing; it was all muscle memory. When finished, he stowed the skimmer in the weapons locker, took off his survival suit and hung it next the others.

He softened his knees as he walked back to the mess as the ship began to sway under increased speed, leaving the Hole for new grounds. The target species was squid, another twelve hours south, maybe more. Rickets shivered involuntarily. Squid meant subantarctic islands, which meant cold. He opened the hatch and held it open for Anna and Toby. They stepped through and made their way to their cabin. Some guys just had all the luck, he thought for the second time. He made his way to the gym, where he would no doubt find Rake working out her own flavour of frustration.

Moss slid an elbow against the wall to keep balance as he descended the stairs from the bridge and made his way down another towards the factory. He pencilled an estimate of the haul into his small notepad, waited for the call from the factory foreman to give his estimate to Loos. The number was the same. On the previous trip he and the foreman were seldom that different, Moss gauging from on high, the foreman estimating from looking into the pounds. It was a good haul, twenty-two tonnes, enough to keep the factory busy while they steamed. An independent catch assessment was only one of his jobs. Each trip had its priorities, and the estimate was ranked fourth on this one.

Travelling into the southern squid fishery meant by-catch mitigation was top of list. The subantarctic islands were the breeding grounds for a rebounding sealion population. Prior to mitigation efforts the mammals would be hauled on board regularly, tempted by the net full of their favourite food. SLEDs helped reduce that, sealion elimination devices, an oval grate sewn into the net that allowed the animal to help itself, to a point. The grate stopped them from being trapped in the end of the net, and even offered an escape hatch. Moss needed to check the SLED every time the net was hauled, and keep a look out for heads peeking out of the water. Then there were the petrels and shearwaters and albatross that wanted a piece of the action. The bafflers were tried and tested, but the Battle Ropes needed more study.

Biological work may have been second on the list, but always took the most time. Collect one hundred fish in bins, weigh the bins, then measure and sex each fish. Grab a specimen, lay it out against the measuring tape, record the number on the tablet with a tap of his knife, slice open the gut and check inside. If ovaries were present, decide how far along she was in the cycle. Small and whitish, stage one. Blood vessels present, stage two. Filling with roe, stage three. Fit to burst, stage four. One hundred fish sometimes took a while to process, and on ten occasions the monitor would ask for an otolith. What Moss liked about squid was that they didn't have ear bones.

At the locker room Moss put on coveralls, a hairnet, gum-boots, and ear muffs before descending another set of stairs. The hum of the *Schlosen* filled the factory and skinned fillets were already starting to back up. He watched the new faces at the weigh station, shifting trays, two where Rickets had worked alone, barely keeping up with the pace of the conveyor. They would need to improve. But it was early days. Moss eyed the weight shown above each scale. As it reached the target weight, it was pushed onto the conveyor to the packers. Three or four times a week he would record each weight on twenty trays and get an average, and use his number rather than the vessel's to compute the total amount of fish processed. He left his notebook in his pocket. They appeared to have enough on their minds without the government man auditing their performance.

He walked around the factory, watching the flow of fish and movement of machinery and hands. Moss made a managerial decision. He liked being his own manager. It's not bad being your own boss, he would tell friends, just as long he isn't a dick. Moss thought his boss was a pretty stand-up guy. He told himself to take a look at what was coming out of the pound, make a few guestimates, and take the rest of the day off.

6

"Man, it's cold out here." Lockey rubbed his gloved fingers together in a vain attempt to bring feeling back to them.

"Take off your gloves and stick your hands between your legs," Anna said.

"Playing with myself *would* warm me up."

"Not in front of me," Anna said. "Just do it, it'll work."

"Missing the factory, Lock?" Rickets asked from the other side of the PAC.

Lockey pulled a glove off and blew on his fingers, then removed the other glove. He put his hands between his legs and rubbed them together.

"Hot sarni waiting for you at smoko. An actual toilet. Off shift right on eight hours. No wind and rain." Rickets shook his head. "Shit, I'm making myself miss it."

"Not me," Manu chimed in. "I love it out here."

"Smoko's in the box," Toby said. "All the hot sarnis you ever wanted."

"Pour me some coffee, Rickets," Rake said.

Rickets took off his gloves and pulled a flask out of the box between them. He poured a mug and handed it over. He held the flask towards the others and got no takers, so poured himself a mug and put the flask back. He had to agree with Manu. He didn't miss the factory. It was cold and monotonous most days on the PAC, sitting in the middle of an empty ocean, especially on days like this, but it wasn't a bad way to earn some pay. He sipped the scalding brew and gazed at the horizon, dark and grey and foreboding. It offered a cold and quiet stillness that bore down into his core.

He pointed at the horizon with his mug. "Well, Lock," he asked, "would you trade all this for the factory?"

"Nah," Lockey said. "That tall guy with the funny ears has a pretty cushy gig."

"The observer?"

"Yeah," Lockey said. "Paid to watch others work. Can't be too bad."

"It's a different type of work, that's all," Rickets said. "He just gets a day rate, anyway. No pay when he's off. No catch bonus. No hazard pay."

"Freeze my balls pay, you mean," Lockey said.

"Call it what you want—and that's a good name—it's still pay," Rickets agreed. "This is just another day in paradise."

"Amen," Manu added.

"Keep your watch," Toby chided.

Manu scanned the horizon as the swell lifted the PAC two metres higher, then lost it as it dipped again. He slowly turned his head to the left and then the right and let the sensors in his glasses scan the skies.

"I don't miss it," Anna said. "Especially when it's squid. Too fast, too stressful. Just sorting and packing and noise."

"I like squid," Rake said. "Fast work makes the shift go fast. They're killing it this season."

"So?" Rickets asked.

"Hell no," Rake said. "I've grown too fond of hunting drones to go back to fishing."

"Out here in the great wide open with your man-boy behind you, ready to give you a charge whenever you need it," Rickets said.

"Too right," she said. Rake reached behind and stroked Lockey's leg. "Isn't that the deal, man-boy?" Lockey pulled his leg away blushing, and she laughed.

"Hey Rickets," she asked. "If Lockey's my man-boy, what does that make Anna?"

"Somebody else's girlfriend," he said.

"Good answer," Anna said, smiling at Toby behind her.

"Hey," Rickets added, turning around. "Why are those guys on the bridge such dicks to you?"

Toby pursed his lips and stared back. "They're not that bad," he said weakly.

"Nah," Rickets said before dropping it. "They are."

The PAC reached the farthest extent of its patrol forward and Toby steered it farther south. He took them three kilometres to the south west and slowed, letting the craft climb a swell and pause at the top, seemingly motionless, for a long moment. He looked at Manu, who scanned from side to side. The PAC slid down into the valley between the swell, then slowly raised again. He checked in with the *Cindy*.

"They've set again," he told his crew. "And Loos wants us to move forward sixteen kilometres, so he feels safer." He programmed a course and speed and moved forward, sitting beside Anna. He bent forward and opened the smoko box.

"He does this every day," Lockey said. "Leap-frogging in front of the others."

"And so do we," Toby said. "Every day. Good time to eat. Looks like meat pies. And a Monday surprise, chocolate bars! Pass your helmet, Manu, have some lunch."

"I can wait," Manu said, scanning the far horizon. "You go ahead."

Rickets took off his glove, dipped a hand into the frigid water and flicked drops at Rake. She flinched and shook her head, as if annoyed by a pesky fly. He took more water and flicked it across again.

"Fuck off, Rickets," she said without turning.

An hour had passed since reaching the new search perimeter. Rickets watched the dark clouds on the horizon that surrounded them. Grey was turning to a darker charcoal as the day wore on. He glanced back at Toby, but decided not to ask about any communication from Loos. The captain was no doubt watching the net sensors on his bridge monitor. As the net filled with its precious catch, it expanded, pulling a pin out of a sensor attached to the becket. Three beckets had sensors, activated when that section was full. Three lights were like lining up the fruit in a pokey machine. Skipper was no doubt watching two and waiting for the third before calling it a day. Rickets thought of the speed the squid would flow through the factory, passing through the weigh station, and the poor son of a bitch having to process it all. Did he miss the factory? How did Rake put it? Hell no. He tried to glimpse Auckland Island as the PAC was lifted to the top of swell, but could only see more water. He looked deeper into the darkness of the horizon, but couldn't put a name to what that made him feel.

"Those birds are flying funny." Manu said, interrupting Rickets' thoughts.

"What do you mean by funny?" Rake asked.

"A straight line," Manu said. "Not like they usually do, in that figure eight thing. Maybe they're a different type of bird."

"Magnify," Rake said.

"I'm on full," Manu said, "That's how I saw them. Do you think they're from the island?"

"You see it?" Rickets asked. "Auckland Island?"

"On the horizon," he said, pointing. "Over that way."

"Just pay attention to the birds," Rake said. She lifted her EMP and looked it over. Lockey sat up straighter and put his hand on the charged pulsers beside him.

"I'll take us closer," Toby said. "Give me a target, Manu."

"They're flying that way." Manu pointed his hand slightly off their port, and moved it across to starboard. "There to there."

Toby directed the PAC to where the birds were flying while Manu leaned forward, studying the air.

"Comms from *Cindy*," Toby announced. "They say they pinged something."

"Something?" Rake asked.

"That's all. Stand to, everybody."

"Then those aren't birds, and you know it," Rake said.

"How many do you see, Manu?" Toby asked.

"Five. Ten," he said. "Looks like a little flock."

"Birds?"

"You know what they are. Call it in!" Rake said.

"Tend to your weapon!" Toby snapped, his voice growing higher. "Manu?"

"I ... don't know," Manu said.

"*Cindy*, this is PAC One. Repeat, this is PAC One," Toby said. "You have incoming. Do you read? You have incoming."

"About fucking time," Rake muttered.

Toby ignored her. "*Cindy*, this is PAC One. Do you copy?"

"Roger that, PAC One," he heard in his ear bud. "We're still scanning."

"You don't have to scan, just open your eyes," he replied. "Coming on your starboard!"

"What are their orders?" Rake asked.

"Nothing," Toby said. "They told me to calm down and confirm the sighting."

"Fucking dicks," Rickets said.

"Let's make sure what they are," Toby said.

"We know what they are," Rake said. "Their ping just poked a hornet's nest. Loos is too far south and too far from support. Fucking idiot."

Toby ignored her rant and increased speed. He angled the PAC to get as close to the flock as possible. The PAC raced up the swell, momentarily left the water as it crested the top to splash down on the downward slope, only to race up the next. The crew held onto to the guide lines with one hand and weapons or ammunition with the other. Water stung their eyes as the PAC slammed down again, sending spray over the craft. After five minutes, Toby slowed and rode the crest of a swell as Manu scanned again.

"Drones," he reported, "gotta be at least twenty."

"Be specific," Toby said. "I need numbers."

Manu counted rapidly. "Shit. Twenty. Ish," he added under his breath.

"Rake? Can you do anything?" Toby asked.

"Too far, and they're moving too fast to catch," she said.

"*Cindy*, this is PAC One," Toby reported. "You have incoming, at least twenty drones approaching at bearing zero eight five."

He turned the PAC due west and picked up speed, trying to keep in the bottom of the swell, letting the waves take them in a north west direction. PACs were small and made out of non-reflective material, but he didn't want to risk any chance of detection. He checked their speed and noted the time on his watch. Fifteen minutes at fifteen knots would bring them almost four nautical miles closer. He called to Manu and used his arm to indicate the direction to scan. Anna was already standing by with a skimmer in hand, while Rickets held his weapon ready to raise and fire. On the other side of the PAC, Rake held her EMP similarly, one hand cradling the barrel and the other firmly gripping the stock. Toby caught Lockey's eye and nodded. Lockey grinned back in anticipation.

Toby slowed the PAC and rode to the crest of the swell. Manu leaned forward and moved his head slowly as he scanned the horizon. The rest copied his motion, but saw only grey sea and grey clouds. They descended between swells and Toby motioned with his arm, farther to the south. He steered up the next swell and Manu leaned forward. His view moved to the left then stopped. He tapped his helmet, adjusting the scanner. He slowly lifted his left arm, keeping his head perfectly still, and pointed like a hunting dog. The rest followed his hand but couldn't see anything.

"Eight kilometres," Manu said. "Silhouette of a ship."

"Certain?" Toby asked.

"Definite," Manu said. "Bearing one eight nine true," he added, remembering his training.

Toby relayed the sighting to the *Cindy* while Rickets raised the skimmer to his shoulder and peered through the sight. He programmed the bearings and distance into the weapon.

"Ready when you are," Rickets said.

"Bearing one nine two, distance seven point eight," Manu corrected.

Rickets made adjustments. "Ready," he repeated.

All eyes except Manu's and Rickets' were on Toby. He didn't like the distance, or the lack of visibility, or the swell. The skimmer would announce their presence as well as their location.

"Bearing one nine two, distance seven point seven kilometres," Manu repeated.

"Take it," Toby finally said.

Rickets launched the skimmer, lowered the weapon, and Anna slammed a second missile into the chamber. Manu followed the plume across the water.

"Two kilometres. Three. Four. On course," he reported. "Five—shit!"

"What?" Rickets asked.

"It hit a big swell and ricocheted," Manu said. "Spun off screen."

Toby turned the PAC and shot up the face of a wave and down the next, creating distance from their last location. He slowed at the crest of another wave.

"One nine eight, seven point seven kilometres," Manu said, his voice monotone and factual.

Rickets jerked back as another skimmer shot across the water. Anna slammed a third in and Rickets raised the weapon.

"One nine eight—" Manu started, but Rickets fired a third before he could finish.

"We have incoming," Manu said. "Five birds on their way. Second skimmer wide, a miss. Target bearing one eight nine. Third skimmer intercepted."

"Mother fucker!" Rickets growled.

Manu picked up the ak-ak rifle strapped near his seat and raised it. The boom of it firing deafened all aboard. As the PAC crested another wave Rake fired an EMP. Three drones spiralled downwards. Manu fired again, a pattern of four shots. A drone disintegrated in the air. Rake fired another EMP and the fifth fell into the water.

"Incoming. More this time," Manu said. "I count seven. No, eight."

"Bearings, dammit," Rickets shouted.

"Target bearing one nine eight—" Rickets fired. "They're spreading out. Looks like they're getting smarter," Manu said. "Fourth skimmer intercepted. No hit."

"Bearings!" Rickets shouted.

"Forget it," Toby said. "We're getting out of here."

"Where are they getting all these drones?" Rake asked, but her voice was drowned out by the noise of the engine. She twisted around to see Lockey behind her. He held up three fingers and pointed to the EMP storage box at his feet. She glanced at Anna, who pointed at her ammunition box and held up one finger, then pointed at Rickets and held up another.

"Fuck," Rake mouthed.

"Manu, what's in your box?" she asked aloud.

Manu glanced down. "Four rounds, four in the chamber," he said.

The PAC crested another wave and raced down the other side as Toby angled the craft back towards the *Cindy.* The drones formed a semi-circle, pointed towards the small craft as they grew closer. Once the drones locked on, he knew there would be no way to outrun them. He turned the PAC to starboard, trying to line up the drones, but they spread out.

"Make it count!" he shouted to Rake.

She sighted the nearest drone, counted slowly as it neared, more to calm herself down than measure distance. At four she fired an EMP and the drone spiralled downward, powerless. Booms rang from the ak-ak, and Manu reached down to reload. Two drones flew into the shrapnel and disintegrated. Rake fired a second EMP and another drone fell from the sky. They jerked to the left as Toby veered to port. Rake fired a third EMP as Manu fired two rounds from the ak-ak. A drone was cut to shreds at the same time as it lost power. They jerked to the right as Toby steered to avoid the remaining drones.

Rickets opened the chamber of his skimmer and adjusted the setting. "Heads down!" he shouted and the missile shot out. Two hundred metres away it exploded in a blinding flash. Anna pre-set the remaining skimmer and slammed it into the waiting chamber, while Rake fired her last EMP at the three drones bearing down on them and Manu emptied his ak-ak. Through the debris and smoke a single drone continued relentlessly towards them. Before Rickets could fire his skimmer, the drone dove down and exploded into the PAC.

7

Moss picked up another squid, measured it and held it upside down. He looked at a tentacle, saw a sharp ridge, tapped the male icon and length on his tablet. He picked up another, measured it, saw small round suckers, and tapped the length, and female. Laying it down he ran his knife along the mantel, slicing from the middle to the arrow of the tip. He saw evidence of the ovaries forming, milky fingers running down both sides, and tapped 'stage 2' before dropping the squid onto the conveyor.

Moss was amazed at how little was known about the squid, though the scientists were loath to admit it. On other species there is a stage 5. Once the eggs have been released, the ovaries are spent, waiting to recover to go the cycle again. Squid don't do that—they spawn and then they die. They have a life cycle of about eighteen months. There are no generations to follow, no older tissue samples to test for health or toxicity. No real understanding of spawning locations. An older generation dies and the newer grows and takes its place, only to be replaced again. Year after year, they are still there, still managed, still plentiful, and still profoundly unknown. The quota setting for the species seemed like economics to Moss—three parts magic and two parts wishful thinking.

And yet, they kept coming. They didn't see the catastrophic collapse experienced in the North Pacific fisheries. The coasts of Korea, China and Russia became devoid of the species. It wasn't like the effect of collapse of cod on Canada, which shook that country so profoundly they had instituted a management system which New Zealand copied and improved. Were it not for their insatiable southern neighbour, the Canadians might still have that fish.

"Oh, to be a squid for a day," Moss said, his words lost in the din of the factory.

He picked up another squid and heard an alarm blare four long blasts. He dropped the fish, gathered his tablet and knife and walked out. Factory hands continued working at their stations, but all shot furtive glances towards him and the exit as he hung his apron and started climbing the stairs. The ship lurched violently as he reached the top. He staggered backward and reached out quickly, grabbing the railing and catching himself before he fell. He watched his tablet clatter to the bottom of the stairway, its broken screen staring up at him. Pulling himself upright, he ascended the remaining steps and entered the locker room. He tossed his ear muffs into his locker box, ripped off his rubber gloves and headed out to the stern door.

Deckhands pointed a fire hose up onto the gantry. Moss followed the stream of water and saw a charred rent on the starboard side. A whoomph and a blast followed one after the other as the ak-ak team fired. Moss stepped onto the trawl deck but retreated to the shelter of the walkway as another blast shook the ship. Pieces of the spare nets stored above, along with shards of metal, rained onto the deck. He leapt up a flight of stairs to the winch deck and tried to see what was happening, but the large hydraulic cylinders blocked his view. The cables were groaning under the weight of the net three hundred metres beneath the surface and the ship strained as if trying to get away. Another flight of steps brought him to forecastle deck. Below, deckhands shifted their hose to the burning debris from the last blast.

Off the starboard side of the ship the air vibrated with the sound of drones. Those controlled by crew self-destructed near the incoming swarm, in a suicidal attempt to take out some of the attackers, but the foreign drones were intent on their target. Moss fell against the iron railing as another blast shook the ship. Smoke billowed from the hull and another alarm contributed to the cacophony of sound around him. Grabbing onto the rail to pull himself up, he peered over at the broken porthole the drone had crashed through. He stood up and stared at the scene over the water. Three attacking drones twisted in the air and plummeted into the water. Closer to the stern a crew member set down her pulser and grabbed another as it was handed to her.

She raised it and aimed. Moss followed the barrel as she shouldered the weapon. A swarm of five drones were caught in her sights until they spread out. She fired and one began to spin powerless on its way down. The others flew on, picking a target on the ship. Moss watched as one sped towards him, realising too late that he was the target. He stood like a deer in the headlights as it approached, his hands refusing to release the railing despite every other part of his body wanting to dive to the deck. Time slowed. He could see the rotors turning, the small charges hanging under it, the camera suspended from a gimmel. The thought of a droner on a distant ship watching him through the lens flitted through Moss's mind.

Just as he managed to let go and turn away, the drone was hit by the shrapnel of an ak-ak charge. Shards of plastic and aluminium peppered the deck around him, slicing the exposed skin of his face. He reached up and touched his head, bringing back a blood-stained hand. Hunching down, trying to make himself smaller, he climbed the few steps leading to the bridge, unlatched the door and stumbled into the room. He placed a hand on a cabinet to steady himself and left a bloody print.

Loos glanced at him and then returned his attention to the radio.

"Mayday! Mayday! Mayday!" he called over the mic. "This is the fishing vessel *J. Ardern*. We are under attack and need immediate assistance. Repeat. We are under attack. Coordinates to follow."

"Radio is dead, Loos," Steven said, handing a tea towel to Moss. "Hold that against your head, mate."

"Mayday! Mayday! Mayday!" Loos repeated.

"Drones took out the comms," Stevens said louder. "They're dead. Useless." "Fuck!" Loos answered. Dropping the receiver, he strode the four steps to the controls overlooking the trawl deck. The ship shook with another blast and he grabbed the console to stop from falling.

"Fuck!" he repeated. He activated the third winch to pull the net off the seabed and back to the surface. While trawling, the net acted as an underwater anchor, a drag slowing the vessel.

"Stevens, what's the depth reading?" he called over his shoulder.

"Two eighty-five," Stevens replied. "Twelve minutes, at least," he added.

"Goddammit," Loos said. He grabbed the mic and spoke into it. "Clear the trawl deck. All hands, clear the trawl deck immediately."

Loos flicked open a cover on the starboard winch control, and repeated the action for the port winch. He increased the pitch of the props and the engine protested, vibrating through the levels of decking, and the warp cable let out an audible moan as the tension increased. He turned and looked at Stevens. He shifted his gaze and seemed to notice Moss for the first time.

"Hold onto something," he said.

"What are you doing?"

"The only thing I can," Loos said. "We aren't going any-where with the net holding us."

"Goddammit," he added to himself, looking at the deck below.

He placed his left index finger over the starboard winch release and his right over the port. He breathed in deeply, exhaled, and pressed both fingers down. The winches began to spin rapidly as brakes holding the winches released their hold. The warp unwound, the coil around each winch growing thinner and thinner. The starboard winch played out first. The end of the warp cable leapt from the winch, flying to-wards the stern. The frayed end wrapped around the gantry, grabbing the bridge spanning both sides of the vessel like a desperate tentacle. It held for a brief moment before being yanked off. Railing tore away, smashing onto the deck. The end of the port warp followed, smashed into the damaged gantry. The structure buckled under the sudden onslaught but continued to stand. The end of the warp slammed onto the deck and disappeared with its partner under the waves.

Freed from its submerged weight, the *Ardern* lurched for-ward. Moss flew off his feet and fell to the floor, rising and slamming down again as the bow of the ship crashed through swell. Stevens bent down to check the observer, and helped him to his feet. Leading him to a counter, he handed him a fresh tea towel and guided the man's hand back to his bleeding scalp.

"Hold that there," Stevens said slowly, staring into Moss's dilated pupils. He stumbled over to medical cabinet and grabbed a suture kit and bandages.

"Is he going to live?" Loos asked.

"Yeah, he'll live," Stevens answered.

"Then leave him for now and sort out the comms," Loos ordered. "Get on top and rig something up. Grab some help if you can, and tie yourself to something, because we aren't slowing down."

Stevens put the supplies back in the cabinet and left the bridge. Moss heard his footsteps on the ceiling, pressed down harder on the already soaking tea towel and winced.

"Can you work the radio?" Loos demanded. "I don't need dead weight right now. You can bleed later."

Moss looked from the skipper to the radio and back, gradually making sense of the words. "Sure," he croaked. He stood looking at the radio, holding onto the counter as the ship continued to plough through waves. Moss turned back to Loos, then out the stern windows. Several attacking drones flew towards them, but not gaining any distance.

"Dammit," Loos said, staring at the empty trawl deck and damaged ship.

"Just sit down," he said to Moss. He stepped over and grabbed Moss's arm, guiding him to the couch and pushing him onto it. "Stay there and hold your head," Loos added before walking over to the radio.

"What the hell happened?" Moss asked.

"We got attacked, that's what the hell happened," Loos snapped. He stared at the tall observer, who seemed much smaller sunk into the sofa, bent over and holding his head. He took a deep breath, exhaling noisily. Loos crossed the bridge and sat next to Moss.

"We pinged a ghost ship," Loos said. "Only it wasn't just one. It couldn't have been. There were far too many drones. As soon as we detected any thermal images the first swarm arrived. Then everything happened pretty fast. I'm surprised we're still afloat."

Loos looked at the winch controls, then out the stern window. His eyes followed the ribbon of wake stretching out behind.

A thought scratched at Moss's wounded head, wanting out. "What about the boats?" he said.

"What?" Loos said, suddenly brought back to the moment.

"The PAC's. The boats," Moss asked. "Where are they?"

"I don't know," Loos admitted. "They called in with visuals on the drones. But they're on their own for now. God help 'em." He turned back to the radio, pressing the on-and-off button, with no reward.

"You can't just leave them!"

It came out weak, much quieter than Moss said it in his own head, but Loos heard. He clicked the dead radio again before setting the mic back on its cradle and returning to the couch.

"If we stayed, we were dead," he said. "If we go back, we're dead. Either way, we can't help them. Like I said, they're on their own."

Loos gently placed one of his hands on the tea towel Moss held against his head, and with the other hand lifted Moss's hand away. He lifted the towel up, and set it back down when a flap of scalp lifted away with it. He put Moss's hand back on top of his head and stepped over to the medicine cabinet.

"What I said about bleeding," Loos mumbled as he gathered up the supplies Stevens had put back. "You can stop now."

The ship lurched as it crashed through swell. Loos knelt in front of the sofa and opened the suture kit. He laid out a sterile pad and arranged what he might need – tweezers, scissors, gauze bandages, surgical tape. He stood again and removed the blood-soaked tea towel, tossing it towards the small sink by the coffee machine. It missed and left a red smear on the counter. He pressed on the wound with a sterile pad and Moss groaned.

"You need stitches," Loos said. "But with *Aunty* rocking and rolling I don't think you'd want me doing that."

He reached into the suture kit and removed the skin stapler and placed it next to Moss. Taking more sterile bandages he wiped away most of the blood. Then he took the tweezers, pinched the skin together, placed the stapler where the skin joined and squeezed. Moss shouted as a staple shot out and into his skin. Loos moved the stapler a centimetre and squeezed.

"Ow!" Moss protested.

"I could try to sew this, which would hurt a hell of lot more," Loos said, shifting the stapler and squeezing again. He moved it and squeezed again, and again, until the loose flap was secured to Moss's scalp. Loos rinsed the wound with an irrigation solution, tried to wipe the fluid and blood from the side of Moss's face and taped a bandage over the wound.

"As soon as Stevens is done up top, he'll need to take all those staples out, clean you properly, and close it all up again," Loos said. "But this will do for now." He put a finger under Moss's chin, raised the man's face and looked into his eyes. He took another finger and moved it from left to right. Moss's eyes followed the finger.

"Can you keep an eye on the radio? Send a Mayday if it comes back on?" Loos asked.

"Yeah," Moss said. "I can do that."

Loos went back to the medicine cabinet, returned with a packet of pills and put them in Moss's hand. "These will help with the pain," he said. "Don't take them all at once."

"Thanks," Moss said.

"I'm going to take a look at what those fucking drones did to my ship," Loos said. "Stay here, keep an eye on the radio."

"Aye-aye," Moss replied.

Loos exhaled slowly and shook his head. "Or just sit there and wait for Stevens," he said as he stepped out onto the deck.

8

Rickets gasped as his face broke the surface. He coughed up water, sucked in a breath, and coughed and spat up what he had just breathed in. He moved his arms, to see if they still worked and to stay the right way up. His PFD ensured the latter, as did the survival suit clinging to his skin and making his legs raise to the surface. He stopped flailing and floated. A swell lifted him up, slapped him in the face with cold water, and then lowered him. Water met his gaze until he strained his head around to see behind. The spotter floated nearby.

"Manu!" he called.

Rickets struggled to turn his body and swim towards his crew mate. While flexible and warm when dry, the suits became tight bands around limbs and torso while submerged, ensuring vital core body temperature was maintained. Rickets stopped trying to turn and kicked his feet, propelling himself backwards. His arms tried to help, waving like flaccid fins. A wave lifted him and broke, burying his face in white foam. He coughed again, tried to wipe his eyes and only splashed more water over his face. Craning his neck, he could see the shape of Manu, a blur of red and black.

"Gotcha, mate," he called.

Rickets managed to turn his body before the swell lifted him. He rose, facing Manu, and slid down the other side towards the young man. Manu floated upright in the water, his PFD keeping his head and chest out of the water. His arms drifted out from his body, forming stabilising floats. He grinned at Rickets.

"Gotcha, mate," Rickets said again. "Goddam those fuckers, eh?"

Rickets awkwardly reached a gloved hand over to Manu. His hand rested on Manu's shoulder, giving enough weight to upset the other's balance. Manu flipped forward, his face buried in the cold water, his waist breaking surface long enough for the red stumps where his legs had once been to break the surface. Rickets pulled his hand away and Manu bobbed upright, silently grinning at the PAC-Man.

Rickets flailed backwards, yelling in a sound composed of a collection of no's, or perhaps one long statement of negation, before it dissolved into a primal noise. Manu continued to grin as his body drifted away with the next swell. A shout caught Rickets' attention through the unceasing shouting in his mind, a sound that wasn't from himself.

"Hey!" he tried to answer as a wave hit his face. "Hey!" he tried again. "Over here!"

He listened for a response and heard another shout. He swam backwards towards the origin, trying to kick his feet and push with his hands. The sound grew louder until a hand grabbed onto his shoulder and a face pressed close to his.

"Rickets, thank god!" Toby said. "Are you alright, man?"

"Yeah," Rickets answered.

"Here, grab Anna and keep her between us," Toby ordered.

Toby grabbed Rickets' other arm and made a basket, with the woman secured between them. Rickets gripped Toby's arms and let his legs float beneath them, catching Anna.

"She's bleeding," Rickets said.

"I know, she took a hit to the head," Toby said. "Can you see anything? I've just been trying to keep us together."

Rickets tried to move Anna's hood, but only succeeding in pushing her head back into the water.

"Shit man," Toby growled, "take it easy!"

"What I saw didn't look that bad," Rickets said. "But there's not much we can do about it anyway."

Toby pulled Anna closer to him, which brought Rickets closer too.

"Have you seen the others?" Toby asked.

"I saw Manu," Rickets said. "He's dead."

"Rake? Lockey?"

"I only saw Manu."

Toby brought his face close to Anna's. Rickets couldn't tell if he was crying or just wet. "This is fucked," he said.

"Rake!" Rickets yelled. "Lockey!"

They both listened for a response before Rickets tried again. Only the wind answered. They floated in silence, Anna buoyed between them, lifted and lowered by the sea surrounding them.

Toby broke the quiet. "Activate my PLB, on my shoulder. I don't want to let go of Anna to do it."

"Sure," Rickets said, pulling himself around to the side of Toby and pressing on the locator beacon, cracking the brittle cover and activating the device. He did the same for his own PLB, and Anna's, before grabbing back onto Toby's arm.

"How long till *Aunty* picks us up?" Rickets asked.

"I have no idea," Toby answered.

"What did they say? Where are they at?"

"I don't know," Toby said. "I lost comms after the first wave of drones. I got nothing. They could be anywhere. If they're still afloat."

"Fuck me," Rickets said.

"Yeah, well, not right now." Toby pulled Anna closer, tried to touch her face with a gloved hand, but gave up. He leaned into her and put his face against hers.

"She's cold, man," he said.

"Her face is cold," Rickets said. "So's mine, so's yours. She'll be all right. They'll be here soon."

"You don't know that," Toby said.

"Nah, I don't," Rickets admitted. "So, we'd better help them. Shouldn't these lights go on automatically?"

"No," Toby answered. "They're manual like the PLB's, just in case you want to be hard to find. Like if you're attacked."

"Do you want to be hard to find?"

Toby put his face against Anna's again, tilted his head to be reassured by her breathing. Blood still mixed with the water on her cheek from a wound somewhere under her hood, but it didn't appear to be heavy. He bit her cheek lightly and pulled back, looking for a response. He saw none.

"She needs to be found," he said. "I think we should light up."

"Fifty-fifty, I guess. Our guys or theirs." Rickets asked. "Worth the risk?"

"Your maths is optimistic. That's if anybody is looking. Or around. We don't have anything close to fifty-fifty," Toby said. "Let's light 'em."

Rickets reached across to Toby and hit the light attached to his shoulder. He winced at the brightness and looked away as it began to pulse. He hit his own and saw Toby squeeze his eyes shut before finding somewhere else to point them. Now that the lights were on, he realised how dark it had become. Night was already upon them. Rickets looked at the pocket on the chest of Anna's suit and started to pull off his glove with his teeth.

"I gotta feel your girlfriend up, so don't get mad," he said. The cold bit into his fingers as they probed under the flap and into the pocket. He pulled out small tube.

"Fuck kind of design makes you take your hand out of your glove?" he said. He pointed the finger flare straight up and squeezed. An intense light shot into the sky, bursting into a star above them. Rickets reached into the pocket for the second one, fished it out and held it above them.

"My hand is too cold to squeeze it!" he said.

He felt Toby's bare hand wrap around his and carefully released the finger flare into Toby's palm. The light shot above them and the world went brighter as it exploded. The first flare was just fading as they both tried to pull the next flare from their own pockets. Rickets pulled off his other glove to fire the third flare, exploding in bright light just before Toby's.

"Okay, okay," Toby said. "Save the rest!"

Rickets used his numb fingers and his teeth to put his glove back on, only managing to stretch the material over his fingers, making them useless except as a flipper. He kept his hands on top of the body between them to keep them out of the water.

"Hey man, I think she's coming to," Rickets said.

Anna's eyes flickered open, then squeezed shut as salt water splashed them.

"Babe, wake up," Toby said, blowing on her face in futile effort to dry the water. It succeeded in rousing her enough to flick her eyes open again.

She opened her mouth but no sound came out. Toby blew on her face again.

"Stop that," she protested. "Why's Rickets hugging me?"

"We're in the water," Toby explained. "We got sunk."

"Fuckers," she said. "My head hurts."

"That's a good sign," Rickets cut in. "Means you can feel."

"How's the rest of your body?" Toby asked.

They felt her shift in their arms as she tested her limbs. "Okay," she said. She closed her eyes again.

"No, you don't," Toby said, shaking her the best he could, which wasn't much. "You stay awake now."

"Quiet," Rickets said. "Listen."

All three heads tilted slightly in the direction of a faint hum. As the swell lifted them it grew in intensity, only to diminish as they sank again. As they lifted again the sound seemed quieter.

"Finger flare?" Rickets asked. "Might be Tisha in PAC-2."

"Torch it," Toby said.

Rickets bit the end of his glove and exposed his already numb fingers. He reached into his breast pocket, grabbed the flare, pointed it upward and squeezed. Light shot upward, illuminating the three in the water when it exploded above. It hung suspended for thirty seconds before slowly descending and dimming. The distant hum grew louder, until it became the unmistakable whine of an outboard motor. As the noise grew closer a beam of light passed over the surface, catching the reflective strips on their survival suits. Soon it rested on them, like the scope of a rifle. They turned their eyes away from its bright glare.

Within moments the engine roared close by and the rubber walls of a craft pushed Rickets under the water, dragging Anna and Toby with him. They broke the surface gasping, still clinging to each other. Hands reached down and pulled Anna from the two men's grasp. Her feet disappeared over the side of the vessel and more hands reached over the side, grabbing at their hoods and suits. Both felt themselves lifted into the cold air and then unceremoniously dropped onto the deck. The engine revved and their bodies shifted towards the stern, then rose and fell as the craft struck oncoming waves.

Toby felt for Anna and slid close to her. "Are you okay?" he shouted above the din.

"Yes," she replied. "Who are they? Is this a PAC?"

Rickets rose onto one arm and shifted his knee so that he sat and faced the driver. "Who are you?" he shouted.

The driver lifted his foot towards Rickets and kicked. Rickets' vision exploded into sparks of light and he fell back, his head bouncing against the aluminium decking. He struggled to get up.

"You stay down!" he heard, before another boot hit his head.

Rickets stayed down. His face lifted and fell with the craft, slapping the decking each time. Anna and Toby lay next to him. Rickets tried to move his face, to look upward at the man at the controls, but Toby caught his gaze and very lightly shook his head. Anna reached slowly across the deck to find Rickets' hand. She squeezed it, and kept her hand there. Rickets held on as if it were the last life line he had.

The boat slowed as it neared another, larger, ship. It glistened in the moonlight, the black of the water reflecting off the black of its hull. Lines were dropped from the railing and crew affixed them with d-rings to strong points. A winch groaned as they were lifted out of the water. Toby lifted himself to look at the ship but a foot planted itself on his chest and pushed him down. It stayed where it was, pinning him to the deck. As they neared the gunnels, hands reached over and Toby watched helplessly as Anna was hoisted aboard. Rickets' curse was lost as hands took him by the hood, the shoulder, the hips, any place they found a hold, and lifted him up. He rolled as he was unceremoniously tossed onto the other deck, stopping when he hit Anna's prostrate body. Seconds later Toby fell on top of him.

More hands grabbed them and hauled them to their feet. Rickets glanced at the wooden deck, rust stained railing, nets bundled beside the trawl deck. The main net was fresh out of the water, and emptying into the waiting pound. He lurched against the man supporting him as the ship turned and accelerated. His eyes shot across the ship, taking in what he could in the few seconds available. Two men manned the gantry with what looked like ak-aks. Above them another two stood in the gloom. Another gantry spanned amidship with two men on it. Crates stacked on top of the bridge stored what must be drones and he took in two Droners standing beside them. A mounted missile launcher stood in middle of the top deck, a type he had seen on the naval ships. The radar rotated on its mast, and spun noiselessly in irregular sequence, as if wanting to wobble off. It looked oddly high-tech and out of place on the rusty hulk of a ship that was probably built in the previous century.

Rickets looked at the man standing in front of them. He wore track bottoms and a sweater that was too tight. He was short but muscular. Rickets tried to read the man's eyes and thought he knew the type. He had seen it before, a short man making up for it, with something to prove, especially looking up at Rickets' two metres. The dynamic had led to more than a pub brawl or two in the past. The man's dark face and darker eyes stared back.

"Who the fuck—" Rickets started to say, but a fist to his stomach stopped the question. He bent over, retching, as another hand smacked his head.

"Who the fuck you!" he heard. Rickets fell to a knee as yet another blow struck his head, but the men holding each of his arms quickly pulled him upright.

"I am the second mate of the—" Toby protested. The man supporting him let go long enough to clout him across the head. Toby tried to grab for his throbbing ear but was struck again.

"Who the fuck you!" the man shouted again, before adding something in another language.

Men pushed forward and starting stripping their survival suits off. Rickets felt his arms wrenched as the wet suit was pulled roughly in different directions. He was pushed to the deck and his legs emerged. Hands pulled him up again. He felt more exposed standing barefoot in thermal top and leggings. Toby and Anna stood next to him. The contents of their suits were given to the man with the dark eyes. He took the lights, squinting his eyes in the glare, and tossed them onto the trawl deck. He shouted a command and a crew member scrambled after them, quickly picking them up, shaking them and searching for a way to turn them off. Then the man picked up the remaining finger flare, smiled and pointed it at Rickets. His hand twitched and Rickets flinched. The man laughed.

A crew member handed him the PLBs from each suit. A small smirk crept onto Rickets' face, the corner of his mouth rising slightly. He looked down to hide it, but it was too late. The man stepped over and struck Rickets in the face with his free hand. He shouted, but all Rickets could understand was that it was a question.

"Lights, they're just lights," Rickets answered.

"Fuck you bullshit," the man replied. He dropped one onto the deck and stomped on it with the heel of his steel-capped boot. He picked it up, holding the exposed microchip between his fingers.

"Ahh," he said, shaking his head. "*Ai kwai*!" he said to Rickets. The others around laughed. He stepped over to the rail and dropped the broken locator beacon over. He lifted his arm and threw the remaining two into the dark waves.

He turned and seemed to look at Anna for the first time. His eyes grew wider and he laughed. Walking up to her, he quickly reached out and took her face in his hands. He turned her head to the left and to the right as if inspecting an animal. He followed the blood seeping down her cheek and neck and onto her chest. He grabbed the fabric of her top and tore it, exposing her breasts. Laughing again, he barked a command. She strained against the two men gripping her arms as they pulled her down a companionway and through a door.

Toby strained in the grasp of the men holding him. "Get your hands off her!" he growled. "Hey! I'm talking to you," he yelled.

The man finished watching Anna being half-dragged, half-carried away and the grin on his face faded. He looked at the trawl deck, hopped over a small dividing wall, and picked up a link of chain the size of his fist. He returned to Toby and swung it. Toby's head jerked and his knees buckled. Rickets clenched his jaw, resisting the urge, the need, to do something. Instead, he glared at the smaller man with the dark eyes, who turned towards him expectantly.

"*Mung kit wa mung*," he said to Rickets, in a voice between a whisper and a hiss. "*Gu ja tahmlai mung*." Then he barked a command and both PAC-Men were dragged across the trawl deck, through another hatch to a set of stairs leading to the deck below, and pushed down them.

9

Hands fumbled for the pair and pulled them away from the stairs. Rickets surrendered and let them. They were gentler than the hands-on deck. The ceiling passed by as he slid across the smooth flooring, until it gave way to a doorway. He entered a room and was left lying on the floor next to Toby. He watched several pairs of feet retreat to the other side of the room, where they stopped. The men belonging to the feet sat down. Rickets looked up at their faces, thin and brown. One moved his mouth in what must have been speech. Rickets reached carefully up and felt his head with a hand, wincing as he touched his sore ear.

The one who had spoken moved closer to Rickets. "You okay? You hurt?" he asked in heavily accented English.

"I don't know," Rickets answered. Rickets surveyed his body, testing muscles and joints from his neck down. They all seemed to work, albeit painfully. He rolled to his side and looked at Toby.

"Shit," he said.

Rickets groaned as he sat up. He gingerly felt Toby's head, trying to remember the week of first aid he had received in PAC training. That felt too long ago. The chain link grazed Toby's scalp, so the wound wasn't deep. But deep enough to bleed. Rickets ignored it for the moment and ran his hands down Toby's arms and torso. He reached under him and felt his back, checking his hand for more blood. There wasn't any. Rickets' hands passed over his legs. A knee was scraped, probably from the tumble down the stairs. His thermals were ripped there, so Rickets finished the tear, pulling off the lower half of the garment. He stretched the tube as far as he could without breaking it, wiped Toby's skull with the fabric and then forced it as carefully as he could over the man's head. As bandages went, it was bad, but it was all he had at hand.

"Your friend," the heavy accent said. "He must wake up. He must work."

"Do you have any water?" Rickets asked.

With a gesture, and a few words Rickets couldn't understand, a dented tin mug with brown water was passed to him. Rickets put his nose near and smelled it, drawing back.

"All we have."

Rickets wetted a finger and placed the moisture against Toby's lips. He gently slapped Toby's face. Rickets lifted the mug and let a trickle fall onto Toby's forehead.

"He's out cold," Rickets said.

"That is no good," the man said. "But we steam now. Maybe we have time before next set. Your friend must be ready."

Rickets examined the man. He was young, but wore it like an old coat. He was sinewy, which meant he was strong, but too thin to be called healthy. Rickets placed him from somewhere in South East Asia.

"What's your name?" Rickets asked.

"Tom."

"Tom?"

"No, *Tom*."

"Okay," Rickets said. "What is this?" he asked, pointing up towards the deck.

"This is a fishing boat," Tom explained. "Who are you? Where is your boat?"

"I'm a fisher," Rickets said. "And you sunk my boat." Rickets felt some strength returning and it filled his voice. Tom moved back slowly.

"Not us," he said, showing his hands. "Deck crew," he said, pointing at the ceiling. "They are very cruel. We are workers. Work in the factory."

He saw Rickets' muscles relax and asked, "You Kiwi?"

"Yeah," Rickets said. "Me Kiwi."

"What your name?"

"Rickets."

"Reekit," Tom repeated. He turned behind him and spoke rapidly. Others crowded into the doorway. Rickets heard the words 'Geewie' and 'Zealand' pass amongst them.

"You don't even know where you are," Rickets said, more to himself than those in the room. He turned back to Toby, checked his breathing, saw his chest rise and fall. He took a wrist and searched for a pulse but got nothing. He moved his fingers to his neck and again felt nothing. Rickets shook his head and concluded that a breathing man's heart was most probably beating, even if he couldn't find and feel it. Scuffling towards where Toby's head lay, Rickets leaned against the bulkhead.

"The woman," Rickets asked. "Where would she be?"

"A woman!" Tom said.

"Our crewmate. Short angry man had her taken away," Rickets said. "Where would she be?"

"A woman?" Tom repeated.

"Yes, goddammit!" Rickets took a breath to calm himself. "She was dragged through a hatch. Where can I find her?"

"Pran has his cabin there," Tom said.

Rickets started to get up but was stopped by a shooting pain in his back and several hands holding him down.

"No!" Tom said, "Too many crew. You rest now before next haul."

"Who's this Pran?" Rickets asked.

"He's a bad man. Cruel man. He's First Mate," Tom said. "Very bad man. He'll kill your friend if he is not be able to work. Throw him overboard."

"He'll probably do that anyway," Rickets said. "I need to see the captain."

"No, he's worse," Tom said.

Another thin, sinewy man moved towards Rickets with a damp cloth that smelled as bad as the water in the mug Tom gave him. He showed it to Rickets and pointed at his face. Rickets nodded slightly and the man gingerly wiped at the blood on his cheek and chin before moving to a gash on his shoulder that he didn't even realise was there. Taking the rag, the man dipped it into the mug and moved over to Toby's head, gently wiping at the blood on his face. Rickets scanned the small room. It had four bunks, two at ground level and two above, but each one looked like it slept two or three men. Dirty bedding, mere rags more than blankets, formed several nests on the floor. Rickets' sense of smell, numbed by blows to his head, was returning. Old fish, the sweat of unwashed bodies, raw sewage. A cockroach scurried into a corner.

Rickets opened his mouth to say something, to ask something, but closed it. He sank back against the wall. Tom patted him on the arm, smiled weakly and nodded.

"You rest, Reekit," Tom said. "Close eyes for a moment. Nothing you can do now. I go to the factory. Fish there now. Pran's occupied, but he'll come later."

Pran was occupied, alright, Rickets thought. He wanted to jump up, wanted to save Anna, to get off the ship, but he couldn't do any of those things. Exhaustion held him down stronger than deckhands. And he knew Tom was right. He felt his body lift and fall as the ship powered through swell. He closed his eyes and sank into a black oblivion.

A poke to his ribs brought Rickets awake. He felt another poke. "Wake up, man," Toby said.

"I am," Rickets said.

"They set a few hours ago," Toby said. "Tom thinks they'll haul soon. Says we better be ready."

"Ready for what?"

"Work, he said."

Rickets turned over to face Toby, wincing from the movement. "You look bad," he said to the bosun.

"I feel bad," Toby said. "My left arm tingles, but I can move it more."

"Your face looks lopsided."

Toby reached up with his right hand and felt the left side of his face. "It's numb. Tom tells me it looks better."

"Better than what?" Rickets asked. "You and Anna are going to have matching scars," he added. The impromptu bandage had fallen off to reveal a gash crusted with dried blood and matted hair.

"We have to get her and get out of here," Toby said.

The sound of winches interrupted, a squelching groan that sounded immediately on top of the cabin. The floor vibrated as they began to haul the net up from the deep. Rats scampered out of the doorway when Rickets sat up. What looked like bundles of rags moved and sat up, rubbing their eyes. Men climbed out of bunks. Soon the room was too crowded. Tom pushed through the waking mob to the two Kiwis.

"Follow me and do as I do," Tom said.

"Factory work?" Rickets asked.

"Yes. If many fish, finish them all," Tom answered. "You good with a knife?"

"Oh, yeah," Rickets said. "Where'd you learn to speak such good English?"

"School," Tom said. "Where else?" He glanced at the doorway. "But best not to speak. The less Pran knows the better."

"Come on then," Rickets said, reaching down to Toby.

Toby offered his right hand. Rickets pulled him up slowly, grabbing under his shoulders when he reached his knees and lifting him to his feet. The men in the room filed out and Rickets and Toby followed. They entered a doorway at the end of the corridor. As soon as they were through, a wave of sound and stench hit them. The engine throbbed below them, conveyor belts rattled from end to end. Heavy metal weights drummed on the deck above, announcing the imminent arrival of the net. They walked past the freezers lining the walls, shelves where trays of fish would be stacked, then frozen into a solid block for boxing and shipping. The frost and ice-covered ammonia pipes feeding the freezers stood against a bulkhead. As this was the only way out of the factory, the whole place became a death trap if the ammonia escaped. All they could do was retreat into the pounds and die there among the already dead fish.

Men filed past the pipes and took up stations. Two stayed back to man the freezer shelves, ready to feed in trays from the packing line. Down the line, some were already prepping the trays. Others readied the weigh station, while two prepared to climb into the pounds once the fish arrived. Another stood beside the large circular band saw used to head fish. The blade spun freely, the usual safety cover removed for a reason Rickets couldn't fathom. Still more gathered around a central station, sharpening knives. Some held short bamboo sticks with metal scoops attached to the end. Rickets and Toby looked for any familiar equipment, such as gloves or aprons, but there were none in sight, and none of the men wore them. They climbed over a moving sorting conveyor and stood beside Tom, barefoot and in their thermals, standing shoulder to shoulder with those around them.

Rickets took the knife offered. He inspected the blade and picked up the remains of a whet stone to sharpen it, thinking more about the First Mate than any fish. Tom ran his eyes over Toby and handed him one of the bamboo rods.

"For insides!" Tom shouted. "Scoop the guts!"

"Yeah, I got it," Toby called back.

Rickets looked at the man, his left arm bent in a pose of rest and practically useless. He turned quickly around as the doors to the pound opened from above. For the briefest moment light streamed in, but it was soon snuffed out by tonnes of fish pouring in from the net suspended above. It was a real grab bag, Rickets judged. Anything they could catch was in it. Barracuda, silver warehou, sea bass, arrowhead squid, ling, stargazer, red cod, ghost shark, a fair mix of rat tail and javelin, and the usual and ever-present spiny dogfish. Another noise chimed in to the cacophony, the grinder, or a mincer. Rickets' eyes followed a conveyor that ran in front of the pounds to the port side of the ship, where a heavy grinder would mince anything fed to it and then eject the remains into the sea. A man at the pounds was throwing handfuls of javelin into it, as well any spiny dog near enough to grab.

"We start! You work!" Tom shouted.

Headed fish started to pass by on the conveyor in front of them. Men grabbed the nearest and sliced them open to remove the innards, or scooped out the headless carcasses. Rickets watched Toby struggle to grab a silver warehou with his left hand before quickly setting down the bamboo rod, using his right hand to stick the fish under his left, and picking the scoop back up to use. Rickets grabbed a ling, sliced it from the anus to the gaping hole where its head had just been, and ripped out the guts. Tom stopped him before he dropped it into the chute leading to the packing conveyor beside them.

"The swim bladder!" Tom called. "Cut and remove. Keep there!" he added, pointing with his knife to a tray.

Rickets pinched the white swim bladder between the fingers of his left hand and sliced it off with the knife in his right. He washed it off in the sea water pumped down a channel at knee height and tossed it into the bucket before grabbing another ling carcass and repeating the process. He had been told years before that the bladders were dried and processed for their collagen content, then put into make-up or face creams for women wanting to feel or look younger. After a trip where they targeted ling, he almost threw up the first time a heavily made-up woman at a pub leaned over to kiss him. All he could see were fish guts on her face.

He tried to focus rather than drift off as he typically did with mindless work. He counted the men below; twelve at the by-catch table, another four at the pounds and mincer and head saw. Another four packing, two at weigh stations and another two at the freezer. Twenty-four. Eight of the men at the table had knives, and there was a cleaver hanging at the end of the table. But the door on the deck above was closed, and there was only one entrance to the factory—the narrow door they had all come through. Rickets grabbed a star gazer, a tough slimy fish living at the bottom of the sea, whose eyes were positioned on the top of its head. He cut along its neck, following its iron hard head on both sides, making a 'v', then turned the fish over and sliced horizontally. He bent it at the neck and cracked its spine, twisted and tore the head off. He looked for a place to put it, then just tossed it onto the mincing conveyor. He ripped out the guts and dropped the carcass down the chute to the weigh station.

He had no way of gauging the passing of time. Fish blood covered his chest and waist. He bent to rinse his knife and hands in the water jetting by and when he stood Pran was beside him. He held a metre-long bamboo stick in his hand. Raising it quickly, he brought it down on Rickets' shoulder.

"*Leeb glap tham gnang! Leeb glap tham gnang!*" he shouted.

He raised the stick and brought it down again on Rickets' shoulder. Pain shot down his right side. He grabbed the knife tight so it wouldn't fall from his hand.

Pran hissed, staring, eyes wide, at the knife before moving his glare to Rickets' face. "*Tha mung chee meed sai gu eg tee gu kha mung naa!*"

Rickets stood, confused and unable to respond. Pran raised the bamboo stick. It whistled through the air, hitting Rickets' forearm. The knife fell to the deck.

Rickets started to bend to pick it up. "Don't!" Tom said.

Pran glanced at Tom before settling his eyes back on Rickets. *"Mung kit wa mung! Gu ja tahmlai mung!"* Spittle flew from his mouth as he shouted. He raised his bamboo stick again and Rickets flinched. Pran laughed.

"Mung nup waa tai lawl ai falang, geewie!" he said.

Pran looked at Tom, swung his stick and hit him across the head. Tom bent over the fish he was cleaning, scooped it clean, and grabbed another. Pran stepped towards Toby, swung his stick and struck him on the back.

"Ai kwai, geewie!" he laughed, moving his hips. *"Ai kwai!"* he repeated, pumping his hips forward and back.

Pran struck Toby again before moving to another station, his shouts heard clearly over the din.

"What the fuck was that about?" Rickets said.

Tom looked across the factory before replying. "He say he will kill you," Tom answered. "He will. But work now. Just work, or he keep beating you. Or kill you here."

Tom grabbed another fish and Rickets dropped the one he had finished into the chute to take it on its way to the weigh station. He reached for a sea bass, slit it and dropped the guts down the chute towards the mincer conveyor. He watched a large rat jump onto the belt, grab the offal in its mouth, jump off and run away. Rickets didn't look in that direction again as the hours toiled on, fish after fish. When the fish in the pound was as low as the knees of the men working inside, the heavy weights of the net clanked on the deck with a fresh haul. The hatch on the trawl deck began opening to dump the new catch. The men inside quickly jumped out of the pound as another load of fish blocked out the light and tonnes more poured into the hold.

Rickets' feet grew numb in the water sloshing across the deck, a sloshing that grew in intensity as the day wore on. Toby tried to grab the table with his left hand and slipped. The men next to him helped him up, looking nervously for the First Mate. Toby tried to open and close his left hand, managing to make a feeble claw. He leaned against the table while he worked, the support it offered the only thing keeping him upright.

After an eternity the pounds emptied. The men at the mincer and bandsaw used to decapitate the fish took hoses from the wall and began spraying their work area with cold sea water, attempting to wash away some of the blood and guts.

"Come," Tom said. "We go. Work finish."

He hung his knife from a hook, and took Toby's bamboo scoop and did the same, before rinsing his hands in the water coursing down the offal chute. He splashed some on his face and behind his neck. Rickets and Toby tried to copy before the sound of shouting and the smack of the First Mate's stick made them stop and hurry to the factory exit.

They filed down the corridor until reaching their cabin, where the exhausted men collapsed into their bunks or onto the floor where their rags and mats lay. Rickets helped Toby sit down and invited Tom do the same. The ship lurched violently as it manoeuvered away and the swell increased. The three huddled together, and the others listened intently despite not understanding the words.

"We have to get out of here," Rickets said.

"What's your plan?" Toby asked.

"Starts with this," Rickets said, and pulled a knife from under his dirty top.

Tom quickly covered the blade with his hand. Toby smiled.

"Okay, we have a knife against men with rifles," Toby said. "It's a start, at least."

"Better than it was before," Rickets added. "And a storm coming up, from the feel of it."

"Where do the crew muster, in an emergency, like a fire or worse?" Toby asked Tom.

"They go on deck," he said.

"Which one?"

"The trawl deck, at the stern, so captain can see all."

"Perfect," Toby said. "Then we have an escape boat."

"Where?" Rickets asked.

"Pay attention to things, Rickets," Toby said. "The one at the bow, beside the mooring lines and a bunch of other shit. An old IRB, but still inflated."

"You saw that when we were thrown on board?"

"I'm surprised you didn't," Toby said. "Tom, are your freezer men trustworthy? Can we trust them?"

Tom turned and spoke in Thai. Two men came forward and joined them. "You can trust them," Tom said.

"Can they cause an ammonia leak, make it look like an accident? Set off the alarms?" Toby asked. "We need it bad enough to cause a general alarm, but not to kill everybody."

Tom explained. They responded. Tom spoke more. After a few minutes of back and forth the two nodded.

"Tom," Toby said, "I'm going to kill Pran with that knife right there. This could be your chance to take the ship. Or come with us."

Tom pursed his lips, then shook his head. "I have contract," he said. "And money already paid to family. I can't be murderer, or ..."

"Mutineer," Rickets offered.

"Or mutineer," Tom said. "But I can help you leave. With your woman."

"You can ask for sanctuary in New Zealand, Tom," Toby said. "You'll be safe."

"But not my family," Tom said. "All our families. Company knows where they are. Police knows where they are."

"Are you sure?" Rickets asked.

"No choice," Tom said. "Once the contract is signed, we're like a prisoner until it's complete."

"No matter how you're treated, or where you're fishing?" Rickets asked.

"No choice," Tom repeated.

The smell of food cut through the general stench and interrupted further conversation. Two factory hands came in carrying two steaming buckets. The others gathered around and reached their hands in, then returned to their bunks or mats eating what was in their hands. Tom gestured a man with a bucket over, reached his hand in and pulled out what looked like dirty rice.

"Eat," he said. "Only food today."

Rickets looked in the bucket at sticky rice with small pieces of fish that looked plucked from the mincer conveyor and something else he couldn't identify.

"Eat," Tom chided. "You will need it."

Rickets reached in, pulling out a large palmful. He pinched some between his other fingers and placed it in his mouth. He gagged.

"Eat it fast," Tom said.

Rickets did as he was advised, stuffing his mouth full and swallowing, chewing only as aid in speeding it on its way. Toby did the same.

"They're going to punish you, aren't they?" Rickets asked, picking up where they left off.

"No, they blame you," Tom said. "And freezer will look like accident. This is an old boat."

"Come on," Rickets said. "That's bullshit. Come with us. Get out of this hell. The ship might be sunk if it keeps fishing here."

"I tell you," Tom said. "If I go my family will not be safe. And what about them?" He said pointing to the others with a nod of his head. "They still here, still work. You go. Escape while you can. I'll be okay."

Toby stopped Rickets from protesting further by placing his hand on the larger man's leg. The three sat silently, eyes down, watching the space between them.

"How long have you been here, Tom?" Toby asked to fill that space.

"One year," Tom answered. "One year more, then I see land again?"

"You haven't been ashore in a year? How do you supply?" Rickets asked.

"Mothership comes and supplies all vessels," Tom said. "Take fish, drop off new boxes, fuel, food."

"Vessels, did you hear that, Toby?" Rickets said. "Those mullets in Wellington don't know shit. And a fucking mothership. How many vessels, Tom?"

"I don't know," Tom said. "Many. Sometimes many waiting for supplies, far off shore."

"Fuck me," Rickets said.

"That would explain all the drones," Toby added. "Do know how many are near us now?" he asked.

"No," Tom said. "When you were brought aboard all hands were locked below. Maybe the storm will scatter them."

"Let's hope," Toby said. "Are these all Thai boats, Tom? I didn't think their fishery was that advanced."

"I hear lots of languages when the mothership arrives. But mostly Chinese," Tom said.

"You're certain?"

"I don't speak it, but I recognise it."

"Say, Tom," he continued after a pause. "What was that Pran kept yelling at me when he was hitting me and doing ... that thing with his hips?"

"He say, *ai kwai*," Tom said. "He say you are buffalo."

"Buffalo?"

"Buffalo big and dumb. It's a big insult. He is saying you are very stupid," Tom said.

"But he is very stupid, he *kwai*," Tom added, looking at Toby and saying much more with his eyes.

Silence filled the gap once again. Finally, Tom said, "Engines will grow quieter when the island is nearby. We rest until then."

10

Tom shook Rickets. "It is time," he said.

Rickets rubbed his eyes, and regretted bringing his hand close to his nose and face. He reached over and shook Toby. He lay on his left, and drool from the corner of his mouth pooled on deck beneath his face. The bosun looked paler, a shade of grey Rickets associated with death. He shook harder. Toby's eyes opened, the right, followed by the left.

"Okay, I'm up."

"It's time," Rickets said.

Toby rolled onto his back and awkwardly placed an elbow down to lift himself up. He grunted as he pulled himself to a sitting position. "Fucking arm," he said, flexing his hand. He was almost able to close the claw.

Rickets pointed at his face; Toby touched his cheek, then wiped the moisture with the back of his hand. "Numb as fuck," he said.

"We'll get you proper help," Rickets said. "But first things first." He pointed a thumb towards Tom, who waited by the door. "Tom says we're sheltering near some land. It's got to be the Auckland Islands." Rickets hoisted Toby to his feet and they joined Tom at the doorway.

"Soon," Tom said. "When you go upstairs, go left. We'll bunch together, hide you from view."

Toby put his good hand on Tom's shoulder. "Thanks, Tom," he said.

Tom returned his gaze to the corridor. The boat swayed in the swell but the vibrations from the floor were gentle as the engine ran slow. Others in the room began to stand up and crowd towards the door. Rickets counted breaths to keep his mind from playing 'what if', creating back up plans and fantasy scenarios of 'might go wrong'. Usually, it was a way to calm himself, to prepare for any contingency. This time it was only making him nervous. Thankfully, he didn't have to count too high.

A loud continuous alarm deafened him. Before Tom dashed down the corridor, Rickets grabbed him, held him in the briefest bearhug while patting his back, then released him. Tom smiled and nodded, disappearing among the others making their way to the deck. Rickets grabbed Toby by the shoulder of his stained top, more to keep them together than support him. They climbed the stairs with the others, and when they reached the deck turned left as Tom instructed. Rickets glanced over his shoulder and saw the men from the factory clumped together, forming a human shield from the deckhands further astern.

He guided Toby through the hatch through which Anna had been taken. It led to a short corridor with four doors, each labelled for the officer inside. Rickets grabbed his fish knife tightly in his right hand and used the left to slowly turn the door handle of the one marked First Mate. Resistance told him that it was locked. He handed the knife to Toby, who took it in his good hand. Rickets shifted himself as far from the door as possible in the cramped hall and swung his body, bringing all his weight to bear on the door. The wooden frame splintered and the door swung open.

Anna sat on the floor, naked, bound at the wrists to an oil heater fixed to the wall. Purple bruises marked her breasts, her thighs and her face. She stared at them through one eye, the other swelled shut. Toby rushed to her and began to cut the rope binding her wrists. Rickets stepped over to the bed.

Pran lay unconscious, a bottle of vodka next to him. Rickets raised a fist and drove it into the man's head, grabbed him by the hair and dragged him to the floor. He kicked him with the heel of his foot. Before he could punch or kick again, he felt a hand on his arm and turned to see Anna holding the knife.

Rickets couldn't hear her, but he read her lips. "Not you," she said.

She pushed him back and stepped over Pran, straddling his body. She sat on his chest, took his hair in one hand and pulled his head back. With the other hand she stuck the knife under his jaw and drove it up into his head until only the hilt remained. His body spasmed as the blade pierced his brain. Anna jammed the knife harder and the movement stopped. She spat on Pran's face, climbed off, and left the knife where it was.

The three stood for a moment staring at each other before Anna looked down at herself. She stepped to a locker, opened it, pulled her survival suit out and started to put it on.

Toby motioned to the suit, then at he and Rickets. Anna shook her head and shrugged.

Rickets started opening drawers, saw a handgun in one and took it, sticking it into the band of his thermals. He saw tobacco, an old-fashioned lighter, and a can of lighter fluid. He opened the can and started spraying it on the bed.

"What are you doing?" Toby shouted.

"Give them something else to keep busy!" Rickets shouted back.

Turning, he bent down and pulled the knife out of Pran's head. He handed it to Toby, before spraying the body with lighter fluid. He went back to the drawer and removed the cigarette lighter. He opened the lid as Toby and Anna moved to the door. Flicking his thumb, a flame shot up. He bent to the bed and the fluid ignited, spreading flames over the covers and mattress. He backed towards the door, touching the lighter to Pran's corpse as he went. Flames snaked across the body.

Rickets tossed the lighter into the room and followed Toby and Anna as they made their way forward, through another hatch and onto the bow.

Just as Toby had described, an inflatable rescue boat sat in a saddle on the port side. They climbed over piles of mooring line and spare warp cables gone to rust. They placed their hands on the boat, to check it was inflated—and that it was real. It was both. Anna climbed on top of it and unclasped the lobster claw hook attaching it to a winch. As soon as she got down, Rickets pulled on the plastic sheeting covering the boat. Anna and Toby pulled as well, and the tarp gave way. Anna stuffed it into the bottom of the craft.

They stood frozen as the alarm cut off, the sudden silence made even more empty after its continuous blaring. All was quiet except for waves slapping against the bow and shouting from the stern. Every sound seemed magnified.

"What are we going to do now?" Anna asked in a loud whisper.

"Same as before," Rickets said. "Up and over."

Rickets turned towards the hatch they had left. The corridor within flickered with an orange light; the wind hitting the bow funnelled through the hatch and fanned the flames coming from Pran's cabin. Smoke filled the back of the ship and shouts carried forward despite the wind. He turned back to the inflatable boat and began to lift the stern. The heavy outboard weighed it down. He bent his knees and heaved upward, lifting the end of the boat out of its cradle and closer to the railing. Anna and Toby lifted the lighter bow. They edged it closer and another deafening alarm began to sound, a continuous blaring meant to cancel all other noise because it was far more important. Sailors feared fire more than any amount of sea, and the fire alarm had sounded. Rickets let out a whoop and with his final reserve of strength moved the end of the boat onto the rail. He signalled to the bow by waving his arms, got their attention, then mimed pushing and held up three fingers. He gave a thumbs up and raised the first finger.

Anna waved her arms and shook her head. She quickly moved to Rickets and pulled him down to her height.

"Are you fucking stupid?" she stated, rather than asked.

She returned to Toby, took the knife from him and cut three lengths of rope from the nearest piece she could find. She tied one end to Toby's wrist, a simple anchor hitch, twice around and through itself, guaranteed not to slip off. She tied a bowline knot with the other end to a handle at the bow of the boat. She went back to Rickets and tossed a length of it to him before finding a handle in the middle of the craft to tie herself to. Only when she finished did she look at Rickets. She tossed the knife into the boat. Rickets took the pistol and did the same. Anna nodded, and rolled her free hand in a 'hurry up' gesture. Rickets tugged on the line securing him, and satisfied with its connection, raised a finger, followed by another, then a third. All three pushed. The inflatable's aluminium bottom scraped against the rail, tipped as its weight shifted, and fell.

Each leapt over the railing before the craft pulled them into it. The craft slammed into the waves, icy water stabbing into any exposed flesh, which for Rickets and Toby was their entire bodies. Anna pulled the line tying her arm to the hand-hold, reached over the rubber side and heaved herself over, tumbling into the hard bottom. She moved forward, found Toby's line and pulled him closer. His right hand fumbled for purchase as he struggled to get up. Anna grabbed both of his arms, planted her feet against the side and strained backwards. Muscles screamed and threatened to pull, but Toby emerged from the water, slithered over the side and fell into the bottom. Rickets grunted, trying to pull himself over; Anna grabbed under his arms and strained backwards until he fell into the boat on top of her.

Anna pushed him off and went back to Toby. The rope tying him to the boat dug into his wrist. She untied it and held his forearm. His hand lay limply, pointing sharply to the left, clearly dislocated at the wrist. She pushed at different places, watching his face, testing for breaks in any of the bones. He winced, but didn't grimace, her substitute for an x-ray. She took both hand and wrist in her grip and used both her hands to squeeze them together. The snap of joints realigning masked Toby's cry of pain. Anna folded the arm across his chest, quickly tied the safety line to his right hand, and placed that on top of his injured wrist, patting it softly.

Both men shivered in the cold wind.

"Get down in the bottom," she whispered. She lifted the tarp and pushed it at Rickets, who immediately wrestled with it, wrapping it around Toby and himself.

She peered into the darkness, seeing only ink black water and the phosphorescence of waves breaking until the swell lifted them. The fishing vessel glowed from the fire, and lay off to their left as it continued to make progress forward. The glow dimmed quickly as the fire was extinguished, replaced by flashlights scanning the water. A beam swept in their direction and Anna ducked, but the swell took them down and out of sight. Looking over the side again, she saw the lights dance across the water, but far from where they were. She ducked down out of the wind and crouched by the men.

"There has to be supplies in a rescue boat, right?" she asked. "I'll have a look."

Rickets rubbed his legs with numb hands before moving closer to Toby, wrapping an arm around him and stroking the man's back. Anna searched the bow and came back with a waterproof bag.

"Most of what should be in this isn't, but it had one of these," she said, opening a small packet and unfolding an emergency blanket made of heat reflective, thin plastic sheeting. She lifted the tarp and wrapped it around the two men. "It should capture your body heat."

She looked over the side again. The ship was a small point of light, already over a kilometre away. Light played across the water, but from the water itself.

"They lowered a boat," Anna said.

"Fuckwits," Rickets said. "In this shit?"

A steady drizzle began, erasing any sight of fishing boat or search craft. Visibly became no more than a stone thrown by a weak arm. Anna sat down close to the men as the little inflatable rose and fell and was buffeted by the wind. She tucked the flimsy emergency blanket around them as tightly as she could. She turned to the outboard motor.

"What do I have to do to start this thing?" she asked.

She had to bend low to hear Toby. "Look for a fuel line running to a tank."

"There is one," Anna reported. "And a tank, with something in it."

"Old fuel mixed with water," Rickets mumbled.

"Find a bulb and pump it," Toby said. "I should have taught all you guys this stuff."

"I'm pumping it," Anna said.

"Good. Now find a starter button," Toby said.

Anna ran her hands over the engine, pressing anything resembling a button.

"That would need a charged battery," Rickets said to Toby. "You think those jokers charged their batteries?"

"Shut up, Rickets," Toby said. "Honey, you'll have to find a pull cord. A rope with a handle—"

"I know what a pull cord is," Anna said. She reached over the cowling, feeling every corner. "There isn't one."

"That's okay," Toby said. "I know what we can do." He started to shift, trying to get to the engine.

"Fuck," Rickets said. "Stay here. Tell me what you have in mind."

"Take the cowling off," Toby said, "Find the fly wheel, if this model is old enough to have one, and make your own pull cord."

"Yeah," Rickets said. "That's what I thought. And then start it with worthless fuel," he added, forcing himself to his knees.

"Don't give up now, Rickets," Toby said. "This is when we need you."

"Not giving up," Rickets said, "just trying to not jinx anything with positivity."

The wind bit into Rickets' flesh as soon as he left the cover of the emergency blanket. He made sure the blanket stayed tucked around Toby and walked on his knees to the engine.

"We're looking for the clips that hold this cover on," he said. Anna moved above him, found a clasp and loosened it. She looked at the other side and unclasped its opposite. Reaching over the engine she located a third.

"I think that's all of them," she said.

Rickets used his numb fingers to pry open the cowling. It lifted several centimetres and came free, catching in the wind and falling into the water behind them. He watched it float away into the darkness before feeling around the top, eventually locating the fly wheel.

"God damn, this is some old shit," he said to himself.

"What?" Anna asked.

He sat with his back against the motor, trying to shelter from the wind. Rain began to fall, icy pinpricks against his skin.

"I'm so fucking cold," he said.

"What do I have to do, Rickets? You can cry later!" Anna said.

"Piece of rope around that wheel," Rickets said. He lifted his wrist and fumbled at the line tied to it. Anna reached over and untied it, following it to where it was tied to the inflatable and freeing it.

"And?"

"Put it around the wheel, and pull it, spin it."

Anna stood in the swaying little boat. She located the fly wheel and wrapped the length of rope around it. She wrapped the end around her hand and pulled. The fly wheel rotated and the rope came off. Rickets sat below her; his arms wrapped around himself. She felt around the wheel and found a groove. Making a knot in the end of the rope, she wedged it into the groove, wrapped it around the wheel and once again pulled. The engine rotated but failed to start. She tried again, with the same result.

Rickets rubbed his hands, slapped them together, clenched them as tight as he could several times, trying to regain more control of his extremities.

"One more time," he said. "Set it up."

Anna wrapped the line around again. Rickets shifted to his knees, then painfully gained his feet, using the line as a tether to keep him from falling. A large swell lifted the boat and as they descended the wave Rickets pulled. The rope tore loose and he fell back and over Toby. But from the rear he heard the sputtering of the motor.

"Give it some gas!" he shouted to Anna as he tried to climb back to the engine. He heard it rev once, loudly, then settle into a continuous purr. The air filled with fumes. At the rear of the boat Anna sat beside the outboard, hand on the throttle.

"Fuck me," he said. "It worked!"

"Where are we going?" Anna asked.

"Away from them," Rickets said, pointing roughly in the direction of the fishing boat, through now driving rain. "And towards that noise."

Anna leaned forward and listened, pointing the inflatable towards the distant sound of surf. Waves crashed on unseen rocks, a dull roar echoing across the water. Toby struggled under the tarp and managed to sit up.

"Keep the sound to your left," he said. "Don't get too close or we can be smashed on a reef."

"The rain is easing," Anna said. "I can see the cliffs."

They turned and saw a massive rock wall looming ahead, illuminated by the faint light of dawn. As the light slowly increased, the rain diminished, revealing a formidable rock barrier. Even at a distance away the cliffs towered over them. Anna followed the coast south, and then north, forced more by the current and swell and wind than the small outboard. Rock walls emerged on their right, funnelling them forward between hostile shores. They gazed up in awe, their thoughts drowned out by the pounding surf. Anna steered for a point where the rocks seemed to meet, and their escape seemed to end.

Toby slapped the side of inflatable. "That's Adams Island!" he said, pointing at the dark rocky land to the right. "And that's Auckland Island," he added, pointing left. "This is Carnley Harbour. Aim straight for that gap."

Anna steered the course he directed. At the crest of a swell they saw the gap, as welcoming as an open mouth. Surf broke on either side and the raucous call of thousands of birds filled the air. As she drew closer, the swell lifted them, revealing jagged rocks dotting the entrance; the mouth was filled with broken teeth waiting to devour them. The little inflatable lifted again and the strong south west wind pushed them through the channel, waves crashing to either side. She followed Toby's pointing arm and angled south east for a narrow gap between two rocks. The outboard whined in protest as she fought the current trying to sweep them aside. The inflatable rose again, and the swell pushed them through and into the channel. The wind diminished, but the rain returned, harder and more persistent. Anna drew close to the northern side, keeping the crashing surf to her left; always within sight of the eerie glow of the white water, but safely distant.

"Up around a promontory, that way," Toby said, pointing south, "is a supply depot. Camp Cove. It's got everything—radio, heater, blankets, food."

"How do you know this shit?" Rickets asked.

"I spent nine months at the Institute to get my Mate's ticket," he answered. "You have to know this to work down here."

"I'm glad," Rickets said. "Not just a pretty face then." The left side of Toby's face continued to droop, including the skin below the left eye. "How are you holding up?"

"I'm cold," Toby said.

Rickets pointed to the eye. "It looks worse."

"Things are kind of blurry out of that eye," Toby admitted.

Rickets tucked the emergency blanket tighter around Toby's left side, and pulled the tarp over his head to keep it, if not dry, at least a little less wet.

11

"Something's wrong with this, guys," Anna said.

Rain dripped off her hood, ran down her arms and off her gloved hands. She twisted the throttle on the outboard and nothing happened. She twisted it again. Rickets left the shelter of the tarp and lifted the fuel tank, shaking it. He squeezed the bulb on the line, but there was nothing to pump to the engine. He held the can so both Toby and Anna could see.

"Empty," he said.

"Are you sure?" Toby asked.

Rickets shook the tank again. He unscrewed the cap and peered inside.

"Empty," he said again.

"There are oars tucked under the sides," Anna said.

Toby shifted to the middle and revealed an oar stowed where Anna said it would be. Its pair lay on the other side. Rickets unstrapped one and handed it to Anna, taking the other for himself.

"Keep close to shore if you can," Toby said.

"Aye-aye," Rickets said, digging the paddle into the water, trying to keep timing with Anna. Water soaked his hands and he soon lost feeling in them. He looked at the engine, now a weight slowing them down.

"Do we need that?" he said, pointing the oar at it.

"The engine?" Toby asked.

"Yeah."

"For what?" Toby asked.

Rickets set the oar on the deck below him and moved to the engine. He held his hands under his arms trying to grab any warmth that might be there, took them out and rubbed them together. He fumbled with one of the vice-like knobs securing the outboard to the IRB. Anna joined him and loosened one, nudged him aside and loosened the other. Rickets gave it a shove and it fell into the water, quickly disappearing. He leaned over the space and reached his head out over the water, pointing an ear the way they came.

"Motor!" he said. He motioned to the rear with a hand. "Listen!"

The sound became more audible as they drifted. Both he and Anna simultaneously climbed back to their oars and paddled, veering away from the noise and towards the shore. Rickets looked back as a wave lifted them up, but could see only mist and rain despite the dawn light. The drone of another motor continued, louder and closer. He jerked around and steadied himself as a wave broke over the back of the inflatable. Anna dug in with her paddle, trying to straighten the craft as Rickets paddled backward, but the next wave caught them side on. White foam splashed into the inflatable but it remained upright and afloat. Another wave struck and pushed them closer to shore, and before he could shake the frigid water from his face and eyes, Rickets was thrown forward into the craft as it ran aground on shingle. He lay stunned on the bottom as another wave lifted them and slammed them down again. The aluminium bottom screeched as it scraped against stone.

"Get up," Anna called, staggering past him and climbing over the side.

She jumped into the surf and grabbed the inflatable, trying to pull it on shore. Rickets lifted himself over and joined her, his bare feet bruising on the sharp shingle beneath. He heaved backwards, up the shore, his feet feeling like exposed bone grinding against the rock. Another wave threatened, climbing up the bank, but retreated. The drone of the motor carried over the surf, closer, but passing by as it moved down the channel. Anna climbed back into the inflatable, helped Toby over the side and onto the shore. She helped him down and covered him with the tarp.

"Come on," she told Rickets.

She grabbed hold of the guide line at the bow of the inflatable and began to drag it. Rickets lifted himself; he half-staggered, half-fell towards her, before steadying himself on the side. He took the line with her, and together they inched their way from the surf, moving closer to the low scrub above the water line. After a struggle against slippery rocks, incessant rain, and biting cold, they managed to drag the boat to the scrub. Satisfied that it was not visible from the sea, they lifted one side and tipped it over, a small knot of stunted rata creating a narrow doorway. Returning to the beach, they supported Toby and brought him to the upturned boat.

"Get him inside and as warm as you can," Anna told Rickets. "I'm going to look for any dry wood."

Rickets looked up, letting the rain hit his face. He shook it off. "I can do that," he said.

"No, you can't," Anna said. "Your feet are bleeding and you're going die of hypothermia like Toby will if you don't get warm. Now get inside!"

She shepherded both men under the craft, satisfied herself that they were at least out of the rain, and set off through the scrub. She broke off pieces of dead wood, wet on the outside but dry inside. She gathered moss from the bottom of trees warped and shaped by the winds. She froze when she heard the drone of an outboard. Crouching low she searched the water but could see no farther than few metres past the shore. The noise increased, and she heard men's voices, a language she recognised from the ship but couldn't understand. They grew louder, and then they began to fade. When all that was left was the sounds of the waves, and birds, and insects, and rain, she continued her harvest, only returning when her arms were full.

She pushed herself under the side of the boat and set her bundle down at the opening. "I just heard them leaving the channel, heading back to their ship," she said.

She sat next to Toby, examining his face. "He's going to freeze to death without some warmth," she said. "Hand me the lighter."

"I haven't got it," Rickets admitted.

She stared at him, but softened her expression and nodded. "Hand me the emergency bag, there's a starter in it, a bit of flint or whatever and a scraper." She took the bag and dug out a starter. "And I'm serious, Rickets. He's going hypothermic. Take his feet and hold them against your belly, and keep that blanket tight around him. Remember your training, man."

She searched through the pile of branches, selected a particularly rotten one, broke it open and dug out the fibrous inside with the knife. Rickets shifted behind her, moving Toby's feet into place. "Do you still have that gun?" she asked.

"Yeah."

"And is it loaded?"

Rickets withdrew the clip and saw five bullets. "Yeah."

"Give me a round."

Rickets took out a bullet and handed it to her. She used the knife to work off the projectile at the tip, and poured the powder into a little nest of kindling. She struck the flint several times before a spark ignited the powder. Bending low and blowing softly she kindled the small blaze, feeding it twigs and moss. Finally, she placed a wrist sized branch on and it began to burn. Smoke, but also warmth, began to fill the space. Checking that the flame wouldn't melt the rubber of the inflatable, and satisfied the small fire would continue to burn, she readied to leave.

"I'm going to get more wood," she said. "Don't let him sleep, Rickets. Keep him warm, and keep him talking. And don't let this go out. When I get back, I'll look at your feet."

Anna helped Rickets move Toby closer to the small fire, touched his cheek, and went back out into the rain.

Rickets nudged Toby. "She's a keeper, mate," he said.

"Yeah," Toby answered, more a breath than a word.

Rickets moved closer to Toby, tightened the blanket around them both to trap as much body heat as possible. Toby closed his eyes and his head started to sag.

Rickets nudged him again. "Hey, stay with me," he said.

"Hey!" he said again, taking some of the man's skin and pinching it.

"Fuck off," Toby whispered.

"No," Rickets said. "I got my orders. Stay awake."

"Fuck off," Toby said again, but with a little more volume.

"These islands," Rickets said. "Tell me about them. Why are they so goddamned miserable?"

Toby shuddered as he breathed out.

"Come on," Rickets chided. "You said you knew about these rocks."

"They're not miserable," Toby said weakly.

"What are they, then?"

"They're beautiful," Toby said. A faint smile played across his mouth.

"Bugs, rain, wind ..."

"And absolutely no people," Toby said. "Especially like you."

"Okay," Rickets said. "Sounding better. What else."

"Nature, just plain nature," Toby said. "They're a nature reserve. And a marine reserve. Big sea lion nursery. And fur seals."

"And birds?"

"So many birds," Toby said. He closed his eyes. Rickets nudged him again. "All right, all right, I was only resting." Toby shifted slightly. "All those guys that flock behind the ship? They live here. At least a lot of them do."

"Makes sense. They gotta live somewhere," Rickets said.

"Some are snow birds," Toby said.

"Never heard of them."

"You know, people who flee to the tropics at the first sign of winter," Toby said. "The petrel, that little guy spends part of the year in Alaska. Or up in Siberia. I kid you not. About as far away as you can get."

"Smart fella," Rickets said. "Say, why do they have this depot if there's no people?" he asked.

"Sometimes people get stuck out here," he let out a small laugh.

"True that," Rickets agreed. He shifted Toby's feet against his belly, rubbing them one at a time.

"Shipwrecks," Toby said. "This used to be on the shipping route, back when we used wind. The rocks would shred the boat, and then the crew'd starve to death or live on birds and seals until another ship happened to pass by."

"People tried to live here," Toby added. "Eighteen forties or fifties. They brought a town, if you can believe it. Flat pack houses. Bricks. Whatever they might need. They were going to build a whaling station. They lasted a few years before giving up. Bunch of drunks, from what I've read. Trying to escape in any way, maybe thought they'd sail away in a bottle."

"I can see this place driving a guy to drink," Rickets said.

"A group of Māori lived here longer. Some chief brought his people and their Moriori slaves. Lasted about seven years. If you find any flax, it's because they brought it. It's right that only the animals have this place now. It's not meant for people."

Rickets took Toby's other foot and rubbed, moving up the calf, creating friction, gently massaging the muscle. Through the faint light and smoke, he saw Toby smiling.

"And yet, here we are," Rickets said.

"There's a bird I read about," Toby said, "the pipit. A little blue robin. Supposed to be so friendly it will land on your hand. Imagine that. I want to see that guy. And there's parrots down here. Parrots, Rickets. And bell birds. Unbelievable. We're in a veritable paradise, Rickets."

"That we are, Toby," Rickets said. "That we are."

Anna returned and deposited an armful of branches. "What a miserable, godforsaken place," she said.

"That's what we were just talking about," Rickets said.

"You look better," Anna said, peeling her hand out of a glove and touching Toby's face with the back of her hand. "More alive." She felt the left side. "How are you feeling?"

He sat up straighter and smiled crookedly. "Cold. Numb. But better."

"Let me see your feet, Rickets," Anna said.

Rickets slid them out from under the emergency blanket and Anna inspected them one at a time. A deep gash ran along the sole of his left foot, and the heel looked shredded. Layers of skin were torn from both. When they warmed up and blood returned, they were sure to bleed a lot. Anna shifted backwards and unzipped her survival suit, peeling it off her shoulder and to her waist. Rickets averted his eyes away from the yellowing bruises on her chest.

"Hand me the knife," she said.

"What have you got planned?" he asked.

"You'll need something to cover those," she said with her hand out. "Knife."

She took the blade. She stared at it for a moment, her hand shaking so slightly only she noticed, and squeezed her eyes shut. She opened them and cut off each arm of her suit, stuck her bare arms through the holes and zipped the front. Four bruises the size of fat fingers striped her arms below the shoulder. Cutting each sleeve at the elbow, she took the upper part and stretched it over Rickets' feet. She reached under the blanket and took Toby's feet, giving them a firm rub and stretched the lower section of the sleeve over each foot. They fit snugly, the tips of his toes peeking through the wrist.

Pulling a section of tarp as straight as she could manage, she started to slice a length a metre and half long and the same wide. She found the centre and made a cut. Anna handed it to the Rickets.

"Try that," she said. "Put it over your head."

"Poncho," Rickets said admiringly.

"It's a bit small," Anna said. "I can have that one and we'll make bigger ones for you two." She looked at Toby, placed a hand on his arm. The emergency blanket crackled as she ran her hand up and down. "You okay for a few minutes while I use this guy?" she asked.

"Yeah," he answered. "I'll be okay."

"Can you be useful?" she asked Rickets. She smiled with her mouth but her eye, the one not swollen, said something else.

In answer, he moved towards the entrance of their makeshift lean-to.

"Empty that bag and bring it," she added. "There's a stream nearby. It should hold water."

He shook out the few remaining contents of the emergency bag and followed her. The rain lightened as she led him towards the stream. Kneeling, he put his mouth in the cold flow and drank greedily. He filled the bag, raised it and checked the seams.

"Leave it," Anna said. "We'll bring it back when we return."

He followed her to a large rock overlooking the channel. He sat beside her and she shifted closer, taking his arm.

"We have to get him help," she said. "He can't stay here long."

"The depot shouldn't be far," he said. "We can paddle. As soon as it's light tomorrow."

She nodded.

"How are you doing?" he asked.

"No," she said. "Don't make me think of anything except getting out of this place."

"Please," she added.

He studied her face. Her jaw was set and lips pursed. She was determined to stay in one piece as long as she could. He looked over at the water, at the birds tilting and swooping through the clearing mist.

"You wouldn't know it," Rickets said. "But those guys out there are really sensitive."

He turned and saw her still staring ahead, but listening. Her head turned slightly as she watched a bird swoop, almost touch a wing tip to the water, turn and rise again. Another flew into view, made a slight adjustment of feather and darted away into the mist.

"It seems that if you call them mollymawks, they get real upset," Rickets said. "Big babies, if you ask me."

He pointed at one, his finger moving as it glided past. "That one is a Buller's Albatross. You can tell by the grey head. And the beak, see? It's yellow, with the black. If they have a white head and plain beak, they're a white cap."

Anna raised a hand and wiped her eyes. Rickets didn't know if was from the rain or from tears. "Thanks for getting us out of there," she said.

"All Toby's plan," Rickets said.

"Just take it for once," Anna said. "Both of you. Enough of the macho stuff. Just ... thanks."

He squeezed her hand under the poncho as a small blue bird fluttered by, taking an interest in them until its curiosity took it elsewhere. Hey little guy, he thought, I know somebody who would like to meet you. He looked along the bank where it flew and let his eyes travel up the hill behind.

"Fuck me," he said. "And that one up there on some kind of mound, that's one of the big ones. A greater albatross. A Southern Royal, if I'm not mistaken. Wing span wider than I am tall."

Anna breathed out a soft laugh.

"I wonder what they taste like," she said. "I am so hungry."

12

Anna sucked on the bone before tossing it into the little fire. She licked her fingers and belched. Toby smiled at her and tried to wink, but as he could only wink with one eye, his left, the gesture pierced her heart more than warmed it. Despite her best efforts at repression, the image of the man who did it entered her mind, his hand raised to strike. She could see again the lust in his eyes, and the pleasure he gained by the violence. She wondered if the image of his face, blurred by tears and proximity, could ever be forgotten. Making a fist, she remembered instead the feeling of resistance as the blade cut through his muscle and flesh, and the satisfaction that flooded her as she gripped the knife, a satisfaction that both warmed and frightened her.

She smiled at Toby, reached over and touched his face, the right side, and tried to convey love and warmth, or something close, with her eyes. It didn't feel like she succeeded. It would take a while before she could let herself feel again. They had both been attacked by the same monster, and they would both need time to heal. If they survived. She watched the rain through the branches piled against the side of the overturned inflatable, Rickets' attempt at a wall or a screen to keep most of the water, and a little of the cold, out. The channel danced and leapt as the wind howled through the tunnel made by the surrounding cliffs. She tried to pray for calmer weather in the morning, but didn't know how, or who, to pray to.

Rickets sat on the other side of Toby, stripping a blade of flax into thin fibres and rubbing them between his palms to make a length of twine. When he finished, he rubbed the ends of the pieces together to make a longer line. His first lengths were tied around Toby's survival-suit-sleeve moccasins, closing the toes and sealing the ankles. Cutting the emergency blanket in half meant they each had another poncho to wear under the tarp. Poking holes in the side of that, he sewed longer lengths of his flax twine to close the poncho around Toby, as well as tie his swollen wrist to his chest as a makeshift sling. He stuffed bird feathers into his own shoes and worked on the lengths that would tie them closed.

Anna pulled Toby towards her, laying his head on her lap, and stroked his hair. His eyes closed and he breathed softly, asleep almost immediately.

"Your grandma, huh?" she said softly.

"Yeah," Rickets answered. "She was an amazing weaver. One of her *kete* is in the local museum."

"Are you going to make one of those next?"

"Who knows, maybe I will," Rickets said. "Maybe make us a sail."

"God knows we'll need it," Anna said.

"We'll make it. I now have the strength of the albatross," he said, opening his arms. "With mighty wings—"

"Shush, for Christ's sake!" Anna said. "Let him sleep."

"He looks better," Rickets said.

"No, he doesn't," Anna said. "He looks warmer is all." She rested a hand on Toby's head. "Better than this morning," she agreed. "I keep checking his ears for fluid, but can't see anything leaking out. Do you remember that part?"

"A little," Rickets said. "Brain trauma or something like that. Not leaking is good thing, right? That training was too short. I didn't think we'd need to use much of it."

"Neither did I," Anna said.

"He'll be okay," Rickets said. "I think if he was going to die, he'd have taken one of the many opportunities already offered. We'll get to the radio, send a distress, and sit in a warm hut waiting for a heli to pick us up."

"Sure," Anna said. "If the goddamned weather lets us."

"It'll let us," Rickets said. "I put in a word with *Tāwhir-imātea*. As well as *Tangaroa*. Both the god of the wind and the god of the sea. They're on our side—we're the good guys."

"Glad to hear," Anna said. "I'm going to try to rest."

"I'll just finish this length and join you," Rickets said, but her eyes were already closed and she was snoring softly.

At the first hint of light, Rickets kicked away the wall of branches in front of the IRB. Rain fell steadily but the wind was light. He and Anna turned the boat over and dragged it back to the water. Toby sat in the bottom as they timed a wave, pushing the inflatable out. Another swell hit them and the bow tilted up, but they came down on the other side, a little farther from shore, before the wave broke. Rickets and Anna scrambled in and began paddling as the next wave lifted the craft, pushing it back before cresting. They dug in their paddles and rode up each successive wave, catching them before they broke, until they were past the surf.

Rounding the first outcrop of rock, the sound of barking and grunting tried unsuccessfully to drown out the noise of the surf. The shore ahead was filled with sea lions, dozens of cows and pups, lorded over by the beachmaster, an enormous old bull, watching over his harem. He lifted his head as they paddled past. Inquisitive seals swam near, their noses rising from the water before their sleek bodies arched and dove under again.

"He's living the dream," Rickets said.

"That your dream, Rickets?" Toby asked.

"To be big and fat and grumpy, surrounded by barking women and crying kids?" he said. "Absolutely."

He watched the seals twist and turn under the water, diving and reappearing twenty metres ahead in the time it took to make a full stroke of the paddle.

"Actually," he said, "these guys look like they have a funner life. I'm changing my dream. I want to be a seal."

"And give up all the women?" Anna asked.

"That's a tough one," Rickets said. "Can't I have both?"

The water began to ripple as a south west wind blew down the channel. Soon waves slapped against the stern, as if pushing them along. Rickets dug his paddle deep to keep the inflatable on course along the shore. They passed more rookeries, sea lions ignoring the wind and dozing on the shore, or moving up the bank and disappearing into the brush. Then shingle and sand gave way to bare rock, rising hundreds of metres, water pouring from above, the spray of the stream blown away before ever reaching the bottom. Clumps of vegetation clung to the face where birds nested. Rounding the cliff, the land gently sloped back to the sea, and to another beach filled with sea lions. The wind slackened, deflected by the rock face.

"There," Toby pointed with his good hand. "Land over there."

He indicated a sloping beach of loose stone, full of sea lion cows basking in the rays of rare sunshine. The clouds parted, revealing patches of blue sky as the aluminium bottom of the inflatable grated against shingle. They climbed out and dragged the craft above the high-water line. They walked silently past the creatures, each cow over a metre and a half long. They scanned the beach for the male, pleased not to see the owner of the land where they trespassed. The beach finished at a level field of spongy sodden peat and clumps of tussock grass. Anna spotted a structure at the edge of the field where it started to rise. She quickened her pace, only to stop and raise her hands to her mouth. Rickets and Toby limped towards her, stopping where she stood and following her gaze.

All that remained of the hut was the charred floorboards and blackened sections of wall.

Rickets went forward and stood by the remains, nudging a lump of melted plastic and metal with his foot that was probably a radio in a previous existence. He picked it up and tossed it to the side. Twisted metal from the roof lay where it fell, mostly on the floor it had once sheltered. Rickets poked around the flooring that was exposed, found a burnt tin box with its lid fused on. He tossed it beside the worthless radio. Other useless items joined the small pile. Finally, he gave up and walked around the remains of the hut, looking in the tussock. He picked up a piece of wood that still had the original green paint on it. He tossed it by the radio and wiped his hands on his poncho before returning.

"How many of these depots are there?" Rickets asked.

"Three, fully stocked," Toby said. "One at the end of the island, at Ross Inlet. The other up the coast in another inlet."

"How far?" Rickets asked.

"Too far," Toby said. He looked at Anna, still holding her hands to her mouth, as if they were the only thing holding her together.

"But there are other places," he said in a firm voice. "Old depots, old huts. Used by scientists. By the Department of Conservation. For research. They're marked with finger posts."

"What are finger posts?" Rickets asked.

"Sign posts. Markers. You can't miss them," he said. If they're still there, he thought. He turned and scanned the ridges behind them. "See that peak over there," he said.

Rickets nodded. Anna said nothing.

"Anna, that one there," Toby continued. "That's the highest peak on the island, called Mount D'Urville. And there to the north is Cavern Peak. In between the two is a saddle, and on the other side is a disused DoC hut. It won't have a radio, but it'll have a pot belly stove, and some supplies. We paddle across the harbour, below that peninsula, and hike up there," he said, pointing.

"That 'we' with the paddling was figurative," he added when they both failed to move. "You're going to paddle while I sit in the bottom of the boat. Then it's five, maybe six kilometres to the hut. It's on the east side, so we'll have no trouble hitching a ride from a fishing boat." He finished by catching Rickets' eye and tilting his head towards Anna.

"Come on, partner," Rickets said to her. "There's a part of my palm that doesn't have a blister yet." He carefully placed a hand on her shoulder and guided her away from the wrecked hut and back to the inflatable. The seals continued to pay them no heed as they pulled the boat back to the water, climbed in and paddled away.

Rickets dragged the IRB as far up the bank as he could while Anna helped Toby off the beach. It was above the tide mark, but nowhere safe if a gale decided to blow—which one was certain to. He searched around the bottom of the craft and located pieces of line, tied them together and then to the bow. He used the line to pull it farther up. He tied the end of the line to a low-lying rata tree; its twisted branches were like hands asking to hold it. He thought of covering it with scrub, to try to camouflage and hide it, but the others were out of sight already. He looked at the orange rubber craft, a beacon to any, friend or foe, who might pass by. Rickets shrugged and left it. He limped off the jagged rocks of the beach, grateful for the softer wet peat above.

Toby's five- or six-kilometre hike looked like more. The beach gave way to a band of bent and stunted trees, leading to a ledge several metres high, and then hillside sloping upward to another ledge, until reaching the saddle. The top was shrouded in mist, and a stream white with foam cut the scene in two. Rickets looked behind at the inflatable, and watched rain work its way across the inlet. He turned back towards the saddle, bent his head as the rain caught up with him, and worked his way towards the others.

Struggling through the dense woods, they crawled through and under the twisted mass of dense spindly limbs. Rickets used his back and legs to push branches apart, allowing Anna and Toby to slither through. His limbs became entwined and body trapped between branches, content for a moment to lie exhausted in their embrace. But he knew that a moment could easily turn into eternity. He kicked and pushed and pulled, snapping weaker limbs that scratched and tore skin.

They emerged through the thicket onto a tussocky rise that ended in a steep rock face. Exploring its base, they spotted a narrow ledge winding its way up. They climbed with Toby between them; Anna pulled him by the hand while Rickets pushed a foot, all the while maintaining their balance. After an hour they reached the top of the ledge and collapsed, letting the rain fall freely on their faces while the sandflies feasted at will. Rising, they drank at the stream pouring from the saddle and carried on, inching and limping their way towards the top. Clumps of tussock formed handholds as they climbed. After several hours they reached the summit, only realising it by the sudden angle of descent. All was white, shrouded in mist and dusted with snow. Any landmark or goal, finger post or sign post, to the hoped-for hut, were hidden.

Snow that couldn't decide if it were hail stung their faces and arms, denying them any rest. Melting rapidly, the little crystals ran down the men's backs. Anna's survival suit let in frigid water through its many cuts and tears. Movement offered the only respite, however weak, from the creeping chill. She and Rickets put their arms around Toby's shoulders and worked their way down the slope; at times all three sat and slid down steep grades. Hands became numbed beyond pain, refusing to open or close. Mist descended with them as they stumbled on. A distant rasping beckoned them forward, until the sound of surf became louder, the distant murmur turning to steady roar. The wind pushing them forward took the mist with it; as quickly as it had blinded them, it disappeared down the channel.

Before them the dark sea stretched out of the inlet. By the shore stood a small hut, clad in plywood painted green, with a tin roof of red. They staggered towards it. A simple latch formed the only security on the door. Where a padlock would normally be, a finger-sized stick of wood was wedged in the hole. Rickets pulled it out and opened the door. Inside was dark and cold, but it was dry. He went to the shuttered window and opened it, letting light flood the place. Two bunks lined one wall, next to a chest full of rough woollen blankets and an assortment of spare clothes. A cupboard and work bench stood against another wall. Anna opened doors and found tinned goods inside, cans of beans, soup, corn. Each had a coating of rust on the top and bottom. Against the third wall sat a squat little potbellied stove, standing on four short legs. A pile of dry wood sat beside it.

Rickets helped Toby cross the room and sit on a bunk. "I thought you were just making this up, man. Well done," he said.

He took out the knife and cut the twine tying the tarp around Toby, and lifted it carefully over his head as he shivered. Anna came over with a thick blanket. She wrapped it around him and helped him lie down.

"I'll get this fire going." Rickets said.

Anna pulled off Toby's make-shift moccasins and dried his feet as best she could before tucking them into the blanket.

"You should take those shoes off, Rickets," she called.

A delicious smell of burnt wood, and the sound of twigs burning, began to fill the hut. "No way," he said. "I don't want to bleed all over the place."

"There's a first aid kit in the cupboard," she said. "Come on."

Satisfied that the fire had caught, he sat at the end of Toby's bunk and let her tend to his swollen and soggy feet. All colour was gone and they were wrinkled by the constant wet, the skin devoid of sensation. Anna cleaned the cuts and gashes the best she could, dabbed what ointment the first aid kit contained, and bandaged the worst. Once she had finished, she wrapped a blanket around his shoulders. He gazed out the grubby window as Anna removed her dirty and torn survival suit, putting on dry clothes from the box. She came over wearing a checked woollen shirt and khaki trousers that were at least three sizes too big, using Rickets' flax twine as a belt. She wrapped a thick blanket around herself and sat beside Toby, taking his frigid hands in hers. She rubbed them gently, trying to restore some warmth to both of their hands.

Rickets hopped on one foot to the box and selected new clothes. There were few to choose from, and mostly too small, but he didn't complain. He found an old pair of thick work-men's socks at the bottom and carefully slid them on over his bandaged feet. He tossed a second pair to Anna before taking a tin of beans from the cupboard, opening it and setting it on top of the pot belly to heat. He adjusted his blanket before sitting beside the fire, watching the flames through the little door in silence.

13

Moss grabbed the little bag with his prescribed antibiotics in it and made his way out of the emergency room. He finally found the glass doors of the entrance that stood at the end of the corridor, after taking too many wrong turns. His head ached, after having it stapled twice and the staples removed. The doctor said he would have a handsome scar as he shaved Moss's hair around the wound and properly cleaned it. After the captain and the First Mate had punched so many holes in his skin, the doctor opted for surgical super glue. As soon as the doors closed behind him, Moss pulled out a wool cap and gently put it over the ghastly landscape of his scalp. The stitches on his cheek and brow were covered in clean white bandages.

Tumeke pulled up in his ute, reached over and opened the passenger door. As the vessel's shore coordinator, it was his job to arrange all the logistics for the ship—removing catch, reloading stores, ordering any needed parts, and seeing that the observer was cared for. In this case that meant collecting his bags from the ship and ferrying him to the airport. All Moss had to do was make a phone call to his FOS and demand he get the first flight back to Wellington. FOS's are typically helpful, most of them having observed themselves, so Moss didn't have to demand very hard.

They drove the twenty minutes to the airport mostly in silence.

"They patched you up good," Tumeke said.

"That they did," Moss replied, looking out his window.

Tumeke turned on the radio which filled the silence until they reached the terminal. Bags unloaded, they shook hands and the ute drove off. Moss usually felt flat after a trip—weeks of routine, even expansive, beauty replaced by concrete and crowds. This time he felt something else. He clenched his jaw as he waited for the flight, and sat staring at the back of the seat in front of him as he flew to the capital. Outside the terminal he swiped a cab outside the terminal with his Ministry taxi card, and the door opened.

"Bags," he said, the first word he had spoken since check in. The boot of the taxi clicked open and he hefted his gear in.

"McGuire Building, Lambton Quay, Ministry of Fisheries," he said.

The computer plotted the most efficient course and a mechanical voice replied, "Fifteen minutes to McGuire Building, Lambton Quay, Ministry of Fisheries," before the door clicked shut and the taxi quietly hummed away. It smoothly joined the midday traffic and followed the sea to the CBD. Wind was forming whitecaps on the water as it funnelled down the bay into the city. Moss shivered, despite the car being warm.

The taxi pulled over to the curb in front of the Ministry and the door clicked open. "Thank you for using Capital Driverless—" the mechanical voice said.

Moss shut it off by closing the door. He fetched his bags out of the boot, lugged them to the stores entrance, keyed in a code and deposited them inside. He took out his Fisheries' ID and was processed through security. Fisheries were, once upon a time, cobbled together with all the other primary resources. Forestry, agriculture, fisheries, biosecurity, to name a few, all under a single Ministry. They even shared the same building with other Ministries. That was all before the *Eazy* grew in importance, and the industry began to dwarf the others. It was also well before Moss's time.

Using his ID card, he activated a lift to the fourth floor. As the doors opened, Aden, his FOS, was waiting. Aden greeted him with a hug rather than the customary slap on the shoulder or handshake.

"Welcome back, Moss," he said. "Man, we're glad to see you."

"Thanks, Aden," Moss said. "Can I have a word?"

"Yeah, right away," Aden said, "But there's folks who want to debrief you first. Maritime and Navy." He started to shepherd Moss to the privacy booths.

"Aden, can't that wait?" Moss asked. "I really need to talk to you."

"As soon as they're done," Aden said, sounding more like a boss than a concerned friend. "Let me take this off your hands."

Aden took the plastic case containing his Ministry issued laptop, trip journal, emergency GPS, camera and other hardware from Moss. He placed a hand on Moss's back and guided him to the booth. They walked past the long tables of analysts that Moss had never met. Many looked up from their computers as they passed. Some gave a thumbs up or a smile. The floor was an open plan design, revolving around a central island containing the lifts. There were no cubicles or separate offices for managers. At the kitchen area Moss stepped towards the coffee maker, but Aden continued to guide him to a far corner where the interview booths were located. They stopped in front of one; two long seats with high backs, blocking the view of others and offering the only real privacy in the office.

"I'll talk to you as soon as you're finished," Aden said, leaving him.

Two men stood and beckoned Moss to sit at the booth. One wore a crisp Navy uniform, while the other had on a fleece with Maritime New Zealand's emblem embroidered on it.

"Thank you for speaking with us, Mr Cignet," the Navy man said. "We understand that it's been difficult week."

Moss sat. "What is it you want to know?" he asked. He looked across the room, trying to see Aden or another FOS, but found himself alone.

"We'll only take a few moments of your time," the Navy man said. "We're trying to get a clear picture of the events of last Tuesday."

"When your ship was attacked," the Maritime man added.

The Navy man cleared his throat. "First off, I'm Lieutenant Commander Braithwaite, and this is my colleague from Maritime New Zealand, Mr John Tender. As John said, we're trying to gain a clearer picture of the attack on the *J. Ardern*."

"Okay," Moss said.

"The initial report of drone activity," Braithwaite began, "sent by a PAC on patrol—"

"I didn't hear that," Moss interrupted. "I was in the factory."

"So, the first you knew of the attack?"

"It was an explosion," Moss said. "I assume a drone exploding against the ship. No, it was the alarm. I left the factory when it went off."

"And then you went to the bridge?" Braithwaite asked.

"Yeah, well, I got delayed on the way," Moss said, pointing to his face.

"So we see," Braithwaite said. "We're sorry for your injuries."

"Where were you?" Moss asked.

"The Naval escort at that time was screening the *H Clark* and the *Andropov*, east of the Auckland Islands, in Fisheries Management Area SOI." Braithwaite said.

"We're trying to ascertain why the *J Ardern* was where it was," Tender cut in.

"And to learn what we can from your experience on the bridge," Braithwaite added, speaking slower than his colleague. "What was happening on the bridge when you arrived?"

"I was pretty messed up," Moss said.

"But you were there," Braithwaite persisted. "What did you see?"

"The communications were knocked out." Moss closed his eyes and then slowly opened them. "Loos tried to send a Mayday, but comms were dead. He sent Stevens up top to try to fix them."

"And you were then the only one on the bridge with Captain van Loos?"

"Yeah, I was."

"What were his actions then?" Braithwaite asked.

"No," Moss said. "Maybe Stevens was still there. He gave me a rag to hold on my head. Loos said 'dammit' and cut the warp cables loose."

"Severing the connection to the trawl net," Braithwaite said.

"Yeah," Moss said. "Drones were hitting the ship and exploding. So, he cut the warps and the ship lurched forward and accelerated away."

"Is that all you can remember?" Tender asked.

Moss kept facing Braithwaite. The men waited as he closed his eyes for several moments. "Loos said, 'We pinged a ghost ship.'" Moss opened his eyes and looked at Braithwaite. "And he said a PAC called in a visual of the drones."

"You heard captain van Loos say this?" Braithwaite said.

"Yeah," Moss said. "Definitely."

"Did he say which PAC?" Tender asked.

"No, he didn't," Moss said.

Braithwaite opened a file for a moment and closed it. "I wonder if you can tell me, in your role as observer," Braithwaite said, "I understand you try to keep an eye on crew as well as all your other duties."

Moss nodded and Braithwaite continued. "Did you see any indication of, well, relationship difficulties between Captain van Loos and the second mate and bosun, Mr Toby Cooper?"

Moss tilted his head and frowned, unsure of the direction of questioning. "Are they okay?" he asked. "The PACs?"

"Their relationship, Mr Cignet," Braithwaite persisted. "What was it like?"

"I ... I got the impression they didn't like him," Moss said.

"They?"

"Loos and Stevens," Moss said. "They treated him like, well, like dicks, if I'm to be honest."

"Please do," Braithwaite said.

"That's all, really," Moss said. "Dismissive. A bit patronising."

"Do you think it possible that Mr Cooper could have radioed information that Captain van Loos may have been dismissive of?" Braithwaite asked.

"Wait a minute," Moss asked. "Is that what you think happened?"

"We're just trying to put together the pieces," Tender added. "The sequence of events."

Moss shook his head. "I couldn't say about that. Like I said, I was in the factory until the attack started." Moss watched Braithwaite make a small note while Tender stared at him. "What other pieces?" he asked.

"The *J. Ardern* was miles in front of its Navy escort, for one," Tender said. "Were you informed of the decision to do so? In your role you have a right to inquire about any decisions that may affect your safety on board."

"When I asked about fishing strategy," Moss said, "Loos told me the squid were sure to be running off the south east coast of the islands. He wanted a large catch."

"The Auckland Islands," Braithwaite clarified.

"That's right," Moss said. He watched the two men as they shifted in their seats, preparing to rise.

"And the attackers," Braithwaite pressed. "Did you see the ship?"

"All I saw were drones," Moss said. "Lots of drones. Flocks of them."

"Flocks?"

"Whatever you call them. There were a lot."

Braithwaite wrote a note in the folder.

"You didn't answer my question," Moss said. "Are the PACs okay?"

"We received a signal from three PLBs, but those were lost. We also found debris from one of the craft," Braithwaite said. "A search was instituted once the Naval escort reached the area, but later called off due to adverse weather conditions."

"How far away did you detect the PLBs from the wreckage?" Moss asked.

Braithwaite checked the file on the table. "At least thirty kilometres," he said, closing it.

"That means they might still be out there," Moss said. "I know how those things work; I go out with one myself. You have to activate it manually. Which means they might still be out there. Are you resuming the search?"

"As I said, the search was called off due to the weather, a strong front passing through the area, and signal was lost immediately prior to that," Braithwaite said. "The Navy will do everything possible to monitor the situation."

"That's a bullshit answer," Moss said. He clenched his jaw and felt his cheeks begin to tingle. "Loos cut and ran," he said, "leaving those guys out there. Isn't that something you're interested in too?"

"There is no need for that language," Braithwaite started. "But I understand your concern. And, yes, we are, in the capacity we are afforded," he added, but his tone signalled the end of their questioning. "Both the Admiralty, and Maritime New Zealand, are committed to keeping fishers safe, and will investigate to the full any actions that may jeopardise our people at sea."

"Is that a 'yes', you are still searching?"

"We are searching in every way we can at this time," Braithwaite said. "Our resources, as you can understand, are quite stretched. There have been incursions into our Exclusive Economic Zone in the Kermadecs, the West Coast, and the Chatham Rise."

He slid out of the booth and put the folder in his brief case. "We thank you for your time, Mr Cignet."

Aden caught Moss at the coffee machine. He reached into the cupboard and took out a mug, placed it in the machine and made one for Moss. When it was ready, he handed it over and made another for himself.

"They treat you alright?" he asked.

"Sure," Moss answered. "Would have been nice if you were there."

"I know," Aden said. "And I wanted to, but they said they'd prefer to see you alone." He took a sip. "Asking about the attack?"

"Yeah, looking for somebody to crucify from the sound of it," Moss said. "The captain is the prime candidate. But he can hang, for all I care."

"Let's keep it neutral," Aden said. He retreated back to his mug after seeing Moss's expression. "Let's go do this," he said after a moment. "We can bring these."

Moss followed his FOS to the work station. Other FOS smiled at him. Those closer shook his hand.

"Oh, my God," his first FOS, Sandy, said. She got up and put her arms around him. He returned the hug. "Does it hurt?"

"Not as much as when it happened," Moss answered.

His plastic carry case was already opened and his equipment either plugged into a monitor or set beside one. Moss looked at the board keeping track of observers and the vessels they were on, as well as listing those waiting for a contract to go out. Each observer's name was on a magnet that stuck to the board. It was an old-fashioned system, and very low tech, but the FOS liked it and it worked. Moss looked at the list of those waiting, which on most months had at least a dozen, sometimes even more. There were very few names on the board.

"Your tablet is broken," Aden said. "But I downloaded all the data."

"Tablets can break when you get bombed," Moss said. He regretted the comment after seeing Aden's face. His FOS was out of his depth, in uncharted waters. Moss didn't want to hurt the man, just use him. He grabbed an empty chair and dragged it beside Aden's.

"We don't really have to do this, do we?" Moss asked. Review photographs, catch data, protected species interactions. "Everything is there. And everyone seems to know what happened."

He gestured at the board. "Looks like you need observers," Moss said. "I want to go out again."

"I don't think anybody will be going out," Aden said. "They're talking about suspending the program until it's safer. But everybody will get a stipend if that happens, to tide them over."

"Suspend?" Moss asked. "From when?"

"The Director is expected to make a statement early next week," Aden said. "This is bigger than just a rogue pirate ship."

"What does that mean?"

Aden swivelled in his chair, checking that the seats at the work station were as empty as he knew they were. "Just what I've been picking up," he said. "Management meeting with suits. Questions that aren't being asked."

"You're not making any sense," Moss said.

"Maybe I'm not," Aden agreed. "But I've been here too long not to notice. Something behind the scenes. Bigger players.

That will change what we're doing. Is changing. Hell, no active observers since the nineties, for Christ's sake."

"Then get me out now," Moss said. "When's the soonest a boat's going south?"

"I don't really think—"

"Look," Moss said, pointing to the board. "There are two, right there."

"Moss, you need some time. Take it," Aden said. "And those are tagged already."

"Don't tell me what I need," Moss said. "They haven't left yet, so whoever you have for them can stand down."

"That wouldn't be fair, Moss," Aden said.

"Don't talk to me about fair, Aden," Moss retorted, pointing to his head. "I did the second trip after you practically said my job depended on it, which was a shitty tactic, by the way. I need to get back down there."

"Are you going to tell me why?" Aden asked.

"There are people still out there," Moss said. "I don't think we should give up on them. Just give me a ship while you still can."

"How are you going to find them with a fishing boat?" Aden asked.

"I just need to get to SOI, close enough to the Aucklands for a PAC to reach them," Moss said. "If they're where I think they are, where the goddamned navy said they might be—"

Aden watched Moss's jaw clench. He got up and walked to the board, studying the magnets. "You can have the *Swarbrick*, or the *Dae-Hae-29*. They'll both be in Dunedin refuelling and re-supplying for the squid season. Both leave on Thursday for SOI."

"Give me the *29*," Moss said quickly.

"Are you sure?" Aden asked. "*Chloe* is the best ship in the fleet. I'm told the observer accommodation is like a hotel suite."

"Just put my name next to the *29* and give me the brief," Moss said.

"Done," Aden removed a magnet name and placed Moss's below the ship's. He wiped his hands as if he did actual work, or what he did had dirtied him somehow. "If anybody looks into this, we'll both be rather screwed."

"Blame me for any and everything," Moss said.

"Just come back in one piece this time," Aden said. "Give me an hour to get your case together and type up a letter of assignment. Got your flight home booked?"

"Yeah," Moss said. "You'll forward me details for the flight to Dunedin?"

"I'll sort that out before you leave the office," Aden said.

Moss nodded. "Thanks," he said. He reached over and squeezed Aden's shoulder. "It's been nice working with you."

Mel shifted from foot to foot as she waited. The stairs were set against the plane and its door opened. For all its growth, Nelson Airport retained the feel of a small hub. She watched as passengers made their way down the stairs and across the tarmac. She smiled as she saw a tall man with a woollen cap bend down and exit. She could see him thank the steward before he descended. His thoughtfulness was one of the things she loved about him. As soon as he cleared the entrance she was in his arms, leaping off the ground and hanging from his strong shoulders. She kissed him, hard at first, but softer as she felt the bandages against her cheek.

She lowered herself to the ground. "Oh, Moss!" she said, and added a hug.

He stroked her head and pulled her tight, before taking her hand and walking to the baggage carousel. She stood facing him as they waited.

"Oh, Moss," she said again. "What have they done to you this time?" She reached up and gently touched the side of his face and peeked under his cap.

"Oh, my God," she added. "Are you okay?"

"I'm good, babe," he answered. "All patched up."

"Aden called," she said. "He scared the shit out of me. Said you were attacked and that you were in hospital as soon as the ship docked."

"I'm sorry about that," Moss said. "He shouldn't have called like that."

"Damn right he should have called," she said. "That's his job." She hugged him again. "I am so glad you're back. I couldn't sleep, worrying about you."

"I'm sorry, babe," he said, holding her tight.

The first of his bags arrived and he let her go, loading it onto the trolley. Mel looked as he continued to wait. A black plastic case arrived and he loaded it, followed by a big blue waterproof gear bag. He pushed the trolley to the entry doors and increased his pace to keep up with Mel. At their car, she spoke a command and the boot opened. Moss loaded his gear and then joined her in the front.

"Home," she told it, and the car hummed away from the curb and out of the parking lot.

At the roundabout it took the third exit towards Richmond. She stared out the window as they drove. Moss reached over and placed a hand on her leg; she put her own hand on top of his, but continued to watch the bay. The tide was out and the mud flats stretched into the distance. They drove in silence, his hand on her leg and her hand on his, through Richmond and towards Rabbit Island, the car flowing with the afternoon traffic. Motueka was still considered a separate town, but it wouldn't be long before Greater Nelson consumed it. They didn't have to drive that far. The car turned off the expressway, navigating through several streets before taking the ramp to their apartment building garage.

The vehicle parked itself in their allotted bay and the doors opened. Moss stepped out and around to the boot and grabbed his personal bag.

"I assume the other shit is staying in the car?" Mel said.

"Yeah," Moss said.

"Oh, Moss," she said. "What's going on?"

"Can we go upstairs, please?" he replied. "I just need to chill for a while, and probably take some painkillers."

"Sure," she said, turning to the lift.

Moss followed and they rode in silence to the third floor. Mel walked down the hall and stood in front of their door. A light scanned her face and the door opened. Moss entered behind her, set his bag down, and walked to the fridge. He opened it, grabbed a beer and twisted the top off.

"It is so nice being home," he said. He lifted the bottle and took a drink.

"How long are you here for, Moss?" Mel asked.

Moss lowered the bottle and set it on the bench. He tried to smile at her, but only managed a twitch from the corner of his mouth.

"I catch a ship in Dunedin Thursday morning," he confessed.

"Moss!" Mel said. "You told me this was the last trip. You *promised* it was the last trip."

"I'm sorry, babe," Moss said.

"So, you are going out again!" she shouted.

"I have to," he said. He stepped towards her but she backed away.

"Why? Because that Aden asked you? Told you he needed you?" she said. "Well, this might be news to you, Moss, but I need you too."

"It's not that—"

"He's going to get you killed, Moss, can't you see that?" she pleaded. "He's not your friend, you know. He's just trying to cover ships so the fish will keep rolling in."

"No, listen," Moss tried again. "He's actually trying to help—"

"You said this trip was the last and look at what happened," she said. "When he said you were in the hospital, I thought ..."

She let Moss hold her as she cried. Her tears made a dark patch on his shirt. He stroked her hair and his eyes grew moist.

"I know I said that," he said, "that I promised that. But there's people out there, I know it. If they're still out there and alive, I have to try to find them."

She didn't protest, so he continued. "They man the PAC, the boat that runs cover and defends the fishing vessel," he said. "The skipper just cut and ran, leaving them there. Even the Navy have given up. But ... I don't know. I have to try. I feel like I owe them that much."

He felt her shift against his chest, turning her face upward. "I could have used my authority to stop the skipper from even going down there. As soon as he got in front of the escort," he said.

Moss replayed the scene in his mind again, what he should have done, what he could have done. Demand Loos return to the convoy, contact the office; send a message on his GPS, with a reference to Uncle Pete, that the office would immediately recognise as code for 'observer in need of assistance'. Or simply press the SOS button on the device. The fantasy didn't help.

"I swear, this is the last time I go out," he added. "I know I said that before, but I mean it. I'll no doubt get fired anyway."

He kissed the top of her head. "I just need to be sure," he said. "Then I'll even work at the Countdown if I have to."

"It's nice at the Countdown," she said.

"I'll be around so much you'll get sick of me."

He felt her arms tighten as she squeezed him. "You idiot," she said into his shirt. "I'll never get sick of you. I just want you here."

"And I'll be here," he said, "as soon as I find them. Then I'm home for good," he added, hoping it would be true.

"And if you don't find them, Moss. What then?"

"Then I'm home for good, too," he said. "I don't want to spend any more time away from you."

14

Moss took a taxi from Dunedin Airport directly to the ship, phoning the company representative on the way. He was waiting by the port entrance to clear Moss for entry, and took him the rest of the way. The *Dae-Hae 29* was an older boat, one of the oldest in the deep-sea fleet. Its dark blue hull was streaked with rust, as were its gantries. Here and there fresh paint covered older rust, which fought for release, existing for the moment as orange stains. The representative co-opted two Indonesian crew members who were passing by to carry Moss's gear up the gangway and to his cabin. They smiled and complied, nodding hello to the observer.

Moss boarded and made his way to the bridge. The shore representative wanted to get formalities, like the initial meeting, out of the way so he could return to other pressing matters, such as renewing crew work visas, passports, or health checks that may have expired while they were at sea, as well as seeing the stores were all delivered. Moss ducked his head and watched his shins while entering. All the doors had lips at the bottom that liked to bite and scratch, he remembered. Standing up after clearing the hatch, Moss smiled.

"Captain Kim," he said. "I am glad to see you again."

"Michael!" the captain replied. "The pleasure is all mine. Welcome back to our little home," he said in impeccable English.

"Please, call me Moss," he said, knowing the captain never would. "And sixty-four metres is not little," he added.

"Bigger than some, granted," the captain said, "but smaller than most. You'll be pleased to know the bath has been upgraded. Water jets, like a jacuzzi."

"Guys," the coordinator said. "Let's do the meet, and have the greet later."

"Of course," Kim said. "Michael, the form please. You can tell me about your face decorations later."

Moss drew a sheet of paper out of a folder and handed it to the shore coordinator, who filled in the names of those present and their ranks. Moss worked his way through the check-list from memory.

"Safety requirements?" he asked. "Hard hat and high vis, steel-toed boots while on deck?"

"Yes," Kim said. "Let an officer know if you need to go out. Alarms ... anything you hear, come to the bridge. This is your muster station. Your lifeboat will be ..."

"Number one," a young mate said.

"Number one," Kim finished.

"I'll need access to your catch returns," Moss said.

"On the computer there," Kim said. "Ask any officer, they'll help."

"Discard ..."

"Our factory manager will discard nothing without your approval, and you will see any fish to be discarded weighed," Kim answered.

"Any protected species, mammal or bird, I'll need to see, and I'll want to retain the first of any species," Moss said.

"Of course. We'll make room in the cold stores should any unfortunate event occur," Kim answered.

"Factory ..."

"I'll have the manager show you the work station," Kim said. "And the crew will make sure you don't hurt yourself lifting heavy bins."

"I have a Ministry camera I'll be using," Moss said. "All pictures are confidential, Ministry property, and I'll try to get hands only if any of the pictures involve crew processing fish."

"I'm sure that will disappoint them," Kim said. "They like their pictures taken."

Moss smiled and tried to remember the next item on his check list.

"The hazard register is on the computer," Kim said, helping. "All incidents logged. That is correct, is it not?" he asked the mate, repeating the question in Korean.

"Yes, correct," the young man replied.

"Very well," Kim said. "Let us sign this form and let our observer settle into his quarters."

"Ah, I'll just do a quick survey of your safety gear, check expirations dates and all that," Moss said.

"Of course," Kim said. He called the young mate, spoke in Korean briefly, before turning back to Moss. "Sejin will show you everything," he said. "And we'll speak again at dinner."

The checks were brief, as all the gear was well maintained. The ship may have been old, but the survival and emergency equipment were not. Moss took pictures of all the survey dates on the life boats, fire extinguishers, electronic location beacons, and noted the location of life vests, survival suits and the two PACs on board.

Shortly after the tour he stood in his cabin, which was just as small as he remembered. A little desk divided the room, with a small refrigerator directly underneath which prevented him from sitting close to it. The room was as wide as he was tall with a hand slightly raised. If the ceiling were a little higher, it would have been a perfect cube, with all the useful space taken up. Two bunks lined one wall, one on top of the other. He tossed his personal bag on the top. The other side of the cabin contained two wardrobes, and between those sat a plastic bin filled with paperwork, bird specimen bags and other bits and pieces required for work with fish. He placed his blue gear bag on top of it, which made the wardrobes difficult to open.

Moss looked for a place to set the black case containing his Ministry laptop, GPS, locator beacon, trip diaries, calculator, and anything else Aden may have put in. He hefted it onto the top bunk and slid it to the end of the bed. He was aware that he might not be using too much of the gear he carried down from Wellington. Once his hands were empty, he leaned on the bunk and stared out of the one redeeming feature of the room, a small porthole that could be opened to let in fresh air. At the moment, he stared at the old wood of the dock and a forklift shifting pallets of frozen fish into the warehouse opposite. But the view would soon change.

The smell of food and the sound of footsteps filled the corridor. As on his previous trip on the *29*, Moss waited for the knock. When it came he reached over, intending to open the cabin door before the Indonesian galley hand could. Even though the handle was just out of reach of his fingertips, he never remembered getting there first.

"Food," the young man said, bringing his hand to his mouth.

Moss smiled and nodded. "Thanks," he said. "*Dri-mah-kah-see*," he tried in Indonesian.

He had spent weeks on the Korean vessel the previous year and didn't learn very much Indonesian. He wanted to rectify that, but the galley hand was already around the corner and on the stairs that descended to the crew mess; the others he mainly saw in the factory, which wasn't conducive to conversation. Moss left his cabin, took the few steps necessary and entered the captain's mess, or 'salon' as the sign above the door announced. Captain Ji Hun Kim sat at the head of the square table. To his left sat the new chief engineer, Ikchan Woo.

On his first trip with the Koreans, Moss had missed the camaraderie of eating with the crew. On a Korean vessel, as an observer, he was considered a junior officer of sorts, given his own cabin (as they were legally mandated to provide) but further set apart by the eating arrangement. On every ship he had sailed, the captain had seniority, of course, but the Chief Engineer was considered almost a second captain, responsible for keeping the boat and machinery running. Kim motioned Moss in to his seat at his right.

"*Kam-sam-eee-dah*," Moss said. He had learned how to say thank you in Korean.

"A feast to start the voyage," Kim said.

Moss surveyed the table. Each meal felt like a feast on a Korean vessel, at least at the captain's table. Small stainless steel and porcelain bowls orbited a large electric hot plate. The bowls contained an assortment of kimchi, pickled cabbages that Moss shied away from, chillies and garlic, spicy tofu, raw broccoli, spicy pork, spicy beef, assorted spiced fish, several types of meats cooked in several ways. Each man had a small bowl of rice beside them and the obligatory soup. A platter with raw strips of beef sat beside the hot plate. Kim already started grilling more. In the corner of the grill sat a thick steak on its way to medium rare.

Kim indicated to the steak and handed Moss a pair of tongs. "For you," he said.

"Wow, that looks good," Moss said. At home he was mostly vegetarian, and Mel strictly so. At sea, he took what he was offered, especially if tender and juicy.

The ship swayed as it steamed through the swell of the Southern Ocean. The Chief Engineer reached out quickly and grabbed the corner of the grill before it shifted towards Moss. The men smiled, but Kim's faded as he glanced out the door and up the stairs to the wheelhouse.

"Young drivers," he said, shaking his head, and the Chief Engineer laughed.

"Michael has sailed with us before," Kim added.

"You must like the *29*," Woo said.

"Very much so," Moss agreed. "How are you finding it below?"

"She has a fine engine," Woo answered. "Korean built. Very dependable. Makes my life easier."

The ship swayed and the engineer grabbed the grill again. Moss held his tongs against it to stop it slipping forward. The men laughed briefly, but Kim ended it by barking Korean out of the door and up the stairs. After a pause, they laughed again. Moss reached into the grill with his tongs and turned the steak over. The juices sizzled. Moss closed his eyes and breathed in the aroma.

"Beer?" Kim said, pointing to the large fridge standing beside the table.

"Sure," Moss said, taking out a can.

He indicated to the other two. They shook their heads and he poured some into his glass. The engineer slid out of his seat and left the salon, retuning a moment later with two small bottles of Cheongju. Handing one to Kim, he opened his own and reached across to Moss.

"Mixer?" Woo asked.

"Please," Moss said, "*Kam-sam-eee-dah*," he added, as the engineer poured some of the strong rice wine into his beer.

All the Kiwi ships he ever observed were dry, alcohol being the reward *after* the voyage was completed. He appreciated the difference in cultures. Moss took a sip before checking his steak and lifting it onto his plate. The ship swayed suddenly and his beer fell, spilling and running off the table. Moss grabbed it quickly and dabbed at the mess with paper towels.

"Another, get another," Kim said, before barking up the stairs again.

Moss grabbed another beer from the fridge and refilled his glass. He held a finger on the rim to balance it as the ship swayed again. Satisfied it wasn't going to topple, he cut a piece of steak and ate it.

"Michael here sees everything," Kim said to the engineer. "Writes it down or photographs it."

"It's my job," Moss added, chewing.

"Even garbage," Kim said. "Anything in the net, he takes pictures and writes it all down."

"It's called benthic material" Moss explained. "Anything from the ocean floor that doesn't move of its own accord."

"Like?" Kim encouraged.

"Like corals, anemones, sponges, rock," Moss said, "It's part of mitigating damage through bottom trawling."

"That's not all," Kim said, taking a sip of wine. "Even the garbage. Last time Michael was with us he found a bowl, like these," he said, pointing his chop sticks at a stainless-steel bowl.

"It was a little more dented and dirtier," Moss said.

"And the big haul," Kim said, laughing. "Tell the Chief Engineer what we caught."

"A washing machine," Moss said.

Woo laughed, catching a bit of wine before it spilled down his chin.

"That's not the best part," Kim said. "He made us keep it—"

"You can't throw garbage into the sea," Moss protested, "even if you just pulled it out. That's not me, that's Maritime Law."

"But tell the Chief Engineer what you told to me," Kim encouraged.

"I told the captain," Moss said, "that I wouldn't count it against his quota."

The engineer laughed, grabbing the grill as the boat swayed, and Moss got up to get another beer.

Moss scanned the horizon and caught a glimpse of their escort, the corvette *Wainui*. According the radar she was seven nautical miles ahead, leading her little flock to the sub-antarctic. He picked up the captain's binoculars and searched to the south west. Soon, he should see the silhouette of the islands. But they were still too far out. Even with help, the eye could see only just so far before the curve of the earth blinded it.

Crew busied themselves on the trawl deck, preparing the net. He went down and recorded all the details about their SLED, measuring the diameter of each side of the oval, the width of each bar, the size of the mesh of the net. He took photographs of the device from multiple angles. At the little desk in his cabin, he found multiple copies of the form he was meant to fill in reporting measurements, serial numbers, net location, even the size of the hole on top that let the sea lions swim out. Before he even went through the motions with the crew, he copied all the information from a previous form onto a new one and filed it.

After finishing with the SLED, he crossed the deck and admired the PAC. Unlike the PAC on the *Ardern*, this was made primarily of aluminium. It had a cowling built over the bow that would keep it dry. A wheel stood at the console, surrounded by screens. Seats lined the side, each facing outward, each with a screen, and each with handles of weapons.

Moss took a picture of it, letting the PAC-Men think it was part of his job. "Has she ever been wet?" he asked.

The PAC-Men glanced at him and continued their preparations, which looked a lot like polishing weapons.

"A little," he heard from the cabin. A young Korean woman emerged. She was neither tall nor short, with a leanness that betrayed long hours of training.

"You the observer?" she asked.

"Yeah," he said. "Moss. What is that accent?" he asked.

"American, I'm afraid," she said. "I grew up in San Francisco. Korean parents," she added, pointing to her face.

"What brings you down here ...?" Moss asked.

"Name's Tanya. But call me Tan," she said. "And what brings me here? A big fat pay cheque, that's what," she said. "And I get to drive this," she added, smiling at her boat.

"She's a beauty," Moss said. He indicated to the other side of the ship with his thumb. "I've only seen the inflatables, like your little sister over there."

"They're useful," she said. "Where'd you see them last?" She raised her chin, indicating his bandages.

"I was on the *Ardern*," he said.

She whistled, and spoke in Korean to her crew. They stopped polishing and took more notice of him, nodding.

"We got hit down in SOI," Moss said, telling her nothing she didn't already know. "Near the islands."

"I hear the captain cut and ran," she said. "Left two PACs to catch the fire."

"Yeah," Moss said. "Good crew, too."

"What kind of fucker does that?" she asked.

"We were getting hit pretty bad," Moss said. "But I was thinking the same thing. As I held my head together and tried not to get too much blood all over the bridge. He'll pay for it."

"Not enough, I'll bet," she said.

"They never do," Moss said. "Hey, I'm going to have word with Kim in little while. You got a minute to spare now?"

"Sure," she said. "Climb in."

"I can't do that, Michael," Kim said. "You should know better than to ask."

"We'll be trawling close to the islands," Moss said. "And you're well covered by the *Wainui* and your second PAC. A patrol there would even strengthen the screen."

"Even if that were so, you being on it is irrelevant," Kim said. "Besides, you are a Ministry observer. No observer goes on a PAC. Hell, you aren't even allowed to lift heavy bins. They wrap you in as much cotton wool as they can."

"I—"

"And you have no idea of the shit storm I would enter if anything happened to you," Kim added. "Not a slap on the wrist, but my license revoked. This is my livelihood, Michael. Even the vessel contract. A lot of men rely on the *29*."

"I understand that," Moss said.

"And, nobody fishes down here without an observer on board," Kim said. "If you are over there in a PAC, how can you observe here?"

"I can't."

"And then how can I fish?" Kim asked.

Moss resisted the urge to answer quickly. He took a deep breath, trying to slow the conversation down.

"The Ministry is going to suspend the observer program until it becomes safer out here," Moss said. "You're right about the cotton wool, which is why they're shelving us. Ships will get an exemption certificate to continue their operations. If you report my negligence, you'll be given one."

"I don't want to report you as negligent, Michael," Kim said.

"But I want you to," Moss said. "This is my last trip. I'd rather keep my lady than a job. And all I want to do, the only reason I'm down here, is to see if my friends are still alive."

"You think a trip on a PAC will tell you that?" Kim asked.

"I don't know," Moss admitted.

He walked to the windows overlooking the trawl deck. The PAC team were finished with their preparations. The weapons Moss saw being polished earlier were all mounted on the cowling. The little craft bristled with spines like an angry muscular hedgehog. It sat securely in its cradle, tethered to a crane by a lobster claw hook, and fixed to the deck with quick release clamps. Earlier, Moss had watched them practise a rapid deploy—crew kitting up, leaping aboard, and the crane lifting them over the side and dropping them. The PAC splashed into the swell, was momentarily submerged before surging onto the surface and speeding away, returning in a wide arc to repeat the exercise. He counted silently as they moved, one barracuda, two barracuda, not reaching thirty before it was in the water and away. And that was while the *29* was at their steaming speed of eighteen knots, in moderate seas.

"Tan has a well-trained team," Moss commented.

"She has the best," Kim said.

"I spoke to her earlier," Moss said.

"I know you did," Kim replied. "She came to me, arguing your case."

"I shouldn't have—"

"No, Michael," Kim interrupted. "You shouldn't have done that. I understand your motive, but you should have come to me first before undermining my authority."

"I'm sorry—"

"But what is done is done," Kim said, gazing out the window to the deck below. "She is a very determined young woman."

Kim continued to stand, hands clasped behind his back, staring out the window. Moss stood silently beside him, trying to read the captain's profile, and watched yet another bridge burning behind him.

"She is very passionate about what she does, and those who do her work," Kim said. "She thinks it is worth a look, and that is what she will do. She'll look after you."

"Thank you," Moss said.

"Don't thank me," Kim said. "You are putting me in a difficult position." He turned and faced Moss, bowed his head slightly, and took his seat in front of the many displays.

Moss walked to the stairs leading to the officer's quarters below. As he reached the first step, Kim turned his head.

"And Moss," he said, "be safe. Good luck."

15

Moss let the crew member secure him into the chair, cinching each of Moss's straps tight before tending to his own. The chair looked like it belonged more in race car than a boat. Each of the PAC crew took their seats and strapped themselves in, swivelled to face the screens at their stations, and checked that their systems were online and responsive. Tan sat at the controls near the bow. Next to her, gauging from the enhanced view on his monitor, was the spotter. The man worked a touch screen keyboard and the view panned across the water, taking advantage of the added height of the *29*.

The craft vibrated slightly and lifted as the crane moved it out over the water before lowering it. A jolt signalled impact with the water, and Moss's seat swivelled violently as they accelerated.

"Lock that in place," the man next to Moss said.

He turned his seat and loosened a strap just enough to reach Moss's seat when he realised his instruction meant nothing to the observer. Moving Moss's chair until it faced the console, he pushed a lever down and Moss stopped swivelling.

"Thanks," Moss said over the slap of the hull on the waves.

He tilted his head back against the seat to stop it banging against the pad every time the craft rose and fell. He strained his neck to view out the front wind shield. The man next to him reached over and activated the screen in front of Moss, gave a thumbs up and went back to studying his own screen. The Auckland Islands appeared on the monitor, rising and falling with the PAC. Moss turned and nodded to the man, but it was unseen; the other's attention was fixed to his own screen. Moss was told he was sitting next to the Skimmer, but the weapon wasn't shouldered. All hardware was mounted on the hull. He took aim and fired using a monitor and keyboard, as did the Ak-Ak, and the Pulser on board. The only weapons not mounted were the small stack of drones, secured near the stern but operated and controlled by the Droner strapped to her chair next to the others.

As the coast neared, Tan reduced speed and the vessel stopped bucking so fiercely. She covered the course plan with Moss on a detailed map before leaving—access Carnley Harbour through the eastern entrance, reconnoitre the western arm for a short distance, before heading to the castaway depot at Camp Cove. Following that, explore the North Arm for any sign of the missing PAC crews before returning to the *29*. Moss's heart sank when he saw the many inlets and hidden coves of the islands. Tan patted his shoulder as she noticed his expression.

The entrance grew in Moss's monitor as they neared. The hills of the southern island, Adam's, slumped away to the left, while its larger neighbour, Auckland, rose steeply out of the water to its highest point, Mount D'Urville. From there it snaked its way north for almost forty kilometres; added all up, the islands consisted of over five hundred square kilometres of land. Moss concentrated on the approaching shore, rather than the size of the task. The opening of the channel leading into Carnley opened like a great jaw, cliffs rising precipitously on both sides. Clumps of greenery were embedded against the stone face, and water streamed in finger thin falls to the surging sea below. Where the shore sloped away, it was covered in a dense thicket of vegetation. Moss peered closer, realising that the grey he saw was not green topped grey stone, but tightly packed trunks and branches of stunted trees.

"Utilise the thermal imaging if you want," Tan said, swivelling briefly to face him before swinging her chair back into place.

The Skimmer beside him didn't wait to be asked, reached over and pressed a key on Moss's touchpad. The screen changed to shades of blues and yellows and oranges. He pressed another key and the visual returned, gave Moss a thumbs up and turned back to his monitor. Moss re-activated the thermal image, tried to make sense of the vegetation and bright colours, and the shore as dimmer light. He panned his view one hundred and eighty degrees before returning to visual, and reverting to his eyes and looking out the window of the cowling.

Massive cliffs rose at the entrance, dwarfing the PAC as it entered the channel. Water poured from unseen sources, myriad waterfalls streaking the rocky face where birds weren't nesting, too steep and weather-beaten even for them. The channel gradually widened, revealing a shoreline dense with bush. Moss magnified the image until the greenery could be seen as intertwined and dense rata, stunted and shaped by the incessant winds funnelling through towards the sea behind. He switched to thermal imaging, saw bright red and strained at his strapping to get closer to his screen. He remembered to magnify, and watched the shape move quickly through the trees, too fast to be human. Despite their best efforts, not all the islands were pest free. Pig, rabbit, mice, goat and probably even feral cat still evaded poison or trap. Left on the island almost two hundred years before as an emergency food supply, or brought as pets by failed settlers, some persisted. Only the rat had found the conditions too hostile.

"Pig," Moss said, though nobody heard but himself.

The channel continued to widen as they entered. Adam's Island lay to the south, taking more shape as the distance increased. A ridge formed a spine separating the north and south sides of what was actually the rim of an ancient volcano. Tan steered the PAC across what was the caldera, towards a peninsula near the shore of Auckland, before angling down the western arm of the channel. She pointed to the direction of Camp Cove as they passed, continued past until they reached a point where the channel turned to the north, before it dipped south again and into the open sea in the other side of the islands. She cut the speed and her crew analysed their screens.

They shook their heads, or reported, "nothing" in Korean, before Tan turned the PAC and angled towards the supply depot at Camp Cove. Birds began to take an interest in the craft, swooping lower and finally landing on the stern and the cowling, on any protrusion. A crew member left his seat and tried to shoo them away, picking up a gaff and swinging it. The birds lifted, but only momentarily.

Tan angled the PAC towards shore as they approached the depot, cutting the engines when the bow ground onto the beach. Most of the birds lost interest and flew away, but nearby seals barked in protest and humped their bodies away to a safe distance from the intruders. Tan, the Skimmer and the Spotter unstrapped and made their way to the stern. She slapped Moss's fumbling hands away from his straps and released his harness.

"Let's go see if our PAC friends are here," she said.

The PAC engine revved and backed off the shore as soon as they had hopped off. It took a defensive position a hundred metres into the harbour as the four made their way past the suspicious animals. Climbing the bank, they continued across wet ground to the burnt remains of the depot.

"What a waste, eh?" Tan said.

She motioned to the Skimmer to climb the bank behind the charred structure, while the Spotter walked in the other direction, scanning the area with binoculars. Moss noticed their side arms for the first time and glanced about, realising that others that they weren't looking for may be around.

"Doesn't look like this happened too long ago," Tan said. "Theory?"

"No," Moss said. "Who'd do this?"

"Somebody who didn't want it used, maybe," she said. She smiled at him and wagged a finger. "I'm intrigued now," she said. She spoke into a small mic linking her to the PAC.

"Just telling them to stay on their toes," she explained to Moss.

He walked to the depot, bent and ran his hand over the burnt wood, marking his fingers with black. "Cold as," he said. "But not old," he added, showing his hand.

He stepped around the collapsed roof and to a small pile of debris near the corner. He used his foot to nudge a burnt box with its lid fused on. He picked up a piece of wood that still had green paint on it. Underneath lay a melted plastic lump that may once been a radio.

"Tan," he called. "What do you make of this?"

She kneeled by the collection, picking through it. "Useless shit," she said. "But collected after the fire."

"That's what I think," Moss agreed.

"Intrigued and interested," she said. She spoke into her mic again and the two crew returned. Tan asked a question in Korean and they shook their heads.

"Let's take a look up the coast," she said. "If our friends came this way, they may have gone north. There's another depot at the top of the island. It's a hell of a way, but they wouldn't have much choice."

The PAC hauled itself back on shore and they climbed on board before it pulled back into the water. The crew resumed their seats as the craft slowly followed the shore line up North Arm. Moss stayed at the stern, clipping his PFD to the railing. The Skimmer handed him a pair of binoculars, something Moss knew how to use, and he scanned the shore and ridge line through the gliding birds. Sealion rookeries gave way to steep cliffs, before descending to tussock-covered hill sides. The PAC explored an inlet as the harbour branched to the north west, until ending in an impassable tangle of rata and stone cliff.

Tan ordered the ak-ak fired and the sound of birds was silenced by the whoomph and explosion above them. Each worked their monitors, studying thermal images and magnifying visual screens, while Moss scanned with his comparatively feeble binoculars. Another whoomph left the craft, followed by an explosion. Several minutes passed before Tan turned the PAC and made their way back down the inlet. She took them up North Arm, slowing at its terminus and firing the ak-ak. The clamour of nesting birds returned to fill the temporary silence as the crew searched the shoreline and hillsides.

Finally, Tan pointed the craft south around an island that resembled a figure eight, and slowly made their way out of the arm. She hugged the shore line of the peninsula across from the destroyed depot at Camp Cove until reaching its southern tip, where she pointed towards the exit of the harbour. Moss scanned the shore with increasing disappointment and frustration, each small opening in the dense cover bringing its own hope and expectation. He stopped as a speck of orange caught his eye. He tried to focus the binoculars but lost it as the PAC continued moving south.

"Wait!" he shouted, pointing towards the shore.

Inside the PAC fingers tapped touch pads and optics zoomed in. Tan angled the PAC after a cry from inside, accelerating to where Moss pointed. He grabbed the side to steady himself against the rise and fall of the boat as the PAC sped towards the shore. The orange grew larger until he saw it was an inflatable raft pulled up on the bank. He gripped the rail tighter and braced himself as the PAC ground upon the shingle. Tan hurried past, followed by her Skimmer. By the time Moss managed to unclip himself from the safety line and climb over the side, the two were already beside the boat. Tan pulled out scraps of tarp and a length of what looked like twine made from a plant.

She spoke into her mic and a whoomph came from the PAC. Moss flinched with the following explosion, but lifted the binoculars with a smile. He scanned the shoreline before lifting them to see a snow covered peak, and north of that a saddle lightly dusted with snow between it and another peak.

"Okay," Tan said. "This is exciting." She spoke into the mic, and the ak-ak fired again.

"I don't think they're here," Moss said. "Look." He handed her the binoculars. "What's on the other side of that?"

She followed his finger up the steep hillside to the saddle. Handing the binoculars back to him, she walked back to the PAC without speaking, climbed in and accessed a monitor. Moss hurried to join her, leaning over to see a map displayed. He followed the coastline up until he saw one of the many long fingers of water poking into the island, only this one ended opposite of where they were, marked by a hut.

"Buckle up," Tan said. "One more stop."

Moss stayed strapped to his race-car chair as Tan took the PAC out of the channel and along the coast. She swung out almost a kilometre off shore, but still the sounds of the sea breaking against the cliff-lined shore hit them like ak-ak booms. Surf rose against stone face, reaching and grasping upward. Behind it the sea regrouped for another surge but was beaten back again. The shore offered no place to land, making it clear that the island wanted to be left to itself. Breaks in the cliff opened inward, into long inlets splitting the steep hills and winding into the spine of the island. Moss followed the line of the ridge to a large block of stone, looking from the distance like a tomb for a giant. Farther north, Cavern Peak rose out of the sea, like a wave threatening to break, its shoulders covered in snow. Between the ridges lay the inlet they sought.

As at the entrance of Carnley Harbour, the opening to Deep Inlet seemed to swallow the small craft. To the left, the cliff face resembled a broken tooth, and the jagged rocks to the right seemed to bite as the sea lifted and fell. Swell from the wide Southern Ocean pushed them into the jaws as they swept up the inlet. Kilometres of inhospitable shore lined their approach, as they followed its bent course into the island. As the inlet neared its end, Moss magnified the view on his monitor and saw the saddle above. Adjusting the controls, he scanned down the steep hill until it formed a gentler slope, finally levelling before meeting the sea. At the bottom of the hill, two hundred metres from the shore, stood a small hut. A thin tendril of smoke rose from a stove pipe before being whipped away by the wind.

"Let's see who's at home," Tan said.

Moss leaned into his screen as the ak-ak was fired and the charge exploded, echoing in the deep channel. He watched the door. The Skimmer next to him did as well, through the sights of his weapon. The door opened and a small woman, in clothing much too large with a blanket around her shoulders, stepped out. A larger man in clothes too small, wearing a similar blanket, joined her.

"Ha!" Moss shouted; he tried to jump up and fell back into his seat.

The Skimmer reached over to unclasp his straps; Moss pushed himself out, waving his arms and shouting as soon as he reached the stern. Tan drove the PAC onto the steep shingle and he leapt out, falling onto the wet stone. He regained his feet and scrambled up the bank. Anna and Rickets stood on the narrow porch under the eaves. Rickets grinned when he saw the tall big eared observer running towards them. He put an arm around Anna and squeezed her shoulder. "Time to get your man home," he said.

She reached up and placed her hand over his. Moss swept them both up in his arms as soon as he reached them.

16

Rickets took the second bunk in Moss's cabin, after Moss removed all the papers and folders from what was his impromptu storage bench. He piled them on top of the other gear stowed between the wardrobes. Toby and Anna filled a cabin vacated by two young Korean officers. But Kim realised he wasn't merely short of space; he was woefully lacking in medical supplies and expertise. The next morning the Wainui came alongside and Toby was transferred over on a basket slung from a crane. On the other ship he was lifted out and onto a stretcher. The basket returned and Rickets climbed into it, strapped down for the short ride over, his injured foot protruding. Anna followed by ship's ladder.

"I see you are leaving us as well," Kim said, as Moss waited with his personal bag.

"Yeah," Moss said. "I got what I came for." He faced the Korean and gave him his hand. "I want to thank you. You didn't have to do what you did."

Kim laughed. "But you did. I am happy it ended well for some," he said, indicating the PAC-Men.

"I've notified the office, and boxed any equipment for the courier back to Wellington," Moss said.

"Yes, your office contacted me," Kim said. "And issued the exemption as you suspected. It came from the Director herself. She didn't seem too pleased with you."

"It was worth it," Moss said. He moved towards the ladder when the naval rating motioned him forward. "And thank you again,

Captain. It's been a pleasure sailing with you." Moss handed his bag to a rating and gripped the ladder, descending into the tender below, waiting to take him to the corvette.

"Good fishing!" he called to Kim.

"Hi, Anna. My name is Tim Roberts. I'm the ship's doctor. We're glad you're aboard. It sounds like quite the narrow escape." He took a seat across from Anna, placed his hands on his lap and made it clear by the way he relaxed in the chair that he was in no rush.

Anna managed a faint smile. "How is Toby?" she asked.

"Your shipmate, Mr Cooper, will recover," the ship's doctor said.

"My partner," Anna corrected. "Boyfriend … whatever you call it."

"He's taken quite a beating," Roberts said, "but his prognosis is good. I've relieved the pressure in his skull and administered antibiotics, as well a great deal of painkillers. You'll all get a course of antibiotics, as a precaution. And I cleaned and bandaged his many cuts and scratches. You did a fine job with the limited resources at hand, by the way. But he'll need to be evacuated as soon as practicable; he needs to be in a hospital. A helicopter is on its way. I'm assuming you'll be wanting to go with him?"

"Yes," Anna answered.

"Good," he said. "I'll make arrangements, let the folks in Bluff know you're coming. You'll both be cared for much better than on a naval ship." He cleared his throat. "But I think it vital that you are examined now so that any injuries can be initially treated."

Anna looked up at him but didn't speak.

"I've arranged for a female rating to be present during the examination," he said. "Is that okay?"

"Yes," Anna answered again.

"You can say no," he said. "I would understand if you did. But I would highly recommend you get examined as soon as possible."

"It's okay," Anna said. "Now is okay."

He opened the sickbay door and spoke to his clerk outside, then returned to his seat in front of Anna. A moment later a young woman entered and introduced herself. She pulled over a chair and sat next to Anna as the doctor explained what came next.

"I'll first check you for any injuries," Dr Roberts explained. "Then take samples for the lab in Bluff. They may want to repeat the procedure. Is that okay?" he asked.

"Yes," Anna said.

"Your head wound has closed nicely," he started.

Their perch on the forecastle deck offered a grand view of the sunrise. Moss silently handed a stick of gum to Rickets. He unwrapped it, put the gum in his mouth and the wrapper in one of the many pockets of the coveralls. His undersized hand-me-down clothes had been replaced with a grey naval engineer's dungarees that fit him much better. One foot wore a soft soled deck shoe, and the other a plastic gel-boot, ordered by the ship's doctor to ensure the wound on his foot stayed closed. He had kept the woollen cap from the hut, and pulled it down to cover his ears. He nodded because it felt like the right thing to do, started to speak, but stayed quiet as the orange glow on the horizon grew. Pinks brightened as the orb of the sun struggled to rise above the waves and see through a faraway grey.

Rickets shivered. He turned from the new sun and scanned the sea north of the vessel. The lights of another corvette rose and fell as she kept pace with the Wainui.

"Sun rises in the west," he said.

"That it does," Moss agreed.

"But it's … what is our latitude?" he asked.

"Fifty-two, thereabouts," Moss answered.

"So," Rickets said. "Tilt of the earth and all that—"

"And the time of the year," Moss added.

"Of course." Rickets pointed his hand to the left and moved it farther. "Why are we going south west?" he asked.

"Well done," Moss said. "But it's the longitude that you should be asking about."

"Fuck's sake," Rickets said.

"One sixty-eight point twenty. Ish." Moss said. "We keep this up, Campbell Island will rise up out of the sea."

"How do you know this shit?" Rickets asked.

Moss laughed, took out his gum, looked at it, and flicked it into the sea. "You have to think and act like an observer now if you want to know anything."

"Watch people work and count birds?" Rickets said.

"Ha, ha, ha," Moss said. "You be quiet, for one, and you listen and see everything that's going on." He patted Rickets' leg. "You become invisible because you're unobtrusive, and you're an amiable fucker, so people get used to you being there. Act like that, and you learn about the ship. And you can go almost anywhere. Like the bridge."

"You've been to the bridge?"

"Where several screens told me our location and course," Moss said. "And where the captain was taking several calls. Then the Akaroa showed up and we headed towards Campbell."

"Smooth," Rickets said. "Who's fishing down there?"

"Nobody that should be," Moss answered.

Rickets grabbed the stair he sat on as the ship rose and crashed into oncoming wave. A wall of white water flew past as the ship rose again.

"She's like a rodeo horse," Rickets said. "Whatever they're called."

"Which tells you, observer Rickets?" Moss asked.

"That we've sped up," he said. "That somebody's in a hurry."

"You're wasted on a PAC," Moss said. "You'd make an excellent observer."

"Fuck off," Rickets said. "You're supposed to say, 'and why are we in a hurry?'"

"You're just proving me right, Rickets," Moss said. "Let's give it an hour and visit the bridge … maybe, unobtrusively, find out." He rubbed his hands together and blew on them. A bird swooped in the distance, wing dipping down and nearly touching the water before levelling out, tilting, and gliding away from the sea. XWM, white cap albatross, Moss thought reflexively.

"We've got capital now, too," he added. "We should use it while we can."

"Capital?"

"Currency," Moss said. "You've done more than these Navy guys. You sunk a ship. You escaped from pirate fishers. Hell, I rescued a PAC team. Most of these kids probably never fired a gun in anger. Notice how they look at us?"

Rickets pursed his lips and nodded.

"That's capital. Spend it. Use it," Moss said. "While we can. The skipper's name is Lewis, but refer him as Captain, or Captain Lewis. They like their titles in the Navy."

He stood and gripped the rail, watching the grey water race past the grey ship under a grey sky. After a shiver, he headed to the doorway. Rickets followed him to the galley, where there was pot of coffee any time of the day or night. They descended narrow stairs, leaning against the walls to maintain their balance. In the galley, they sat at a long table Moss had seen ratings sitting at. The mess wasn't as rigid as a Korean fishing boat, nor was it as laid back as a Kiwi ship. It was important to know where to sit, or where not. The cook greeted them and poured two mugs. Rickets smiled at Moss and thought of capital.

After a refill, they made their way to the bridge. Moss stepped through the hatch, smiled at an ensign at the radar and stood beside the stern bulkhead. Rickets entered next and stood beside his friend. Captain Lewis glanced over, acknowledged the two with a slight nod, and returned his gaze to the windows facing forward. The view rose and fell as the ship rode the increasing swell. They were well past the roaring forties, and deeper into the howling fifties. In this part of the world the ocean swirled around the pole as it liked, with no land to break its flow except the hapless solitary island that might lie in the way, experiencing the fury of both wind and sea.

Campbell Island was one such place, an uninhabited sub-antarctic island and part of New Zealand's protected Southern Offshore Island fisheries management areas. Like the Auckland Islands, Campbell was a nature reserve, and fishing was closely monitored around its rocky shores. It was ringed by an exclusive twelve-mile zone, and a twenty-five-mile fishing restriction. Moss peered out the window trying to catch a glimpse, but cloud covered any land that might lie ahead. The waters were rich with sea life, but not harvested frequently due to the distance and the high seas. He had never observed this far south, because few chose to go there. It was a simple mathematical formula weighing the cost of the voyage, the risk to ship and crew, and the possible reward. Some had obviously thought the risk worth the effort, Moss thought, as the captain watched the horizon rise and fall through the windows.

Moss tried to read the screens nearby. The radar indicated their bearing as south-south-east. Nothing lay within the twenty-four-nautical-mile radius of its reach, except for the Akaroa on their port flank. He left his place against the wall and stepped towards the thermal imaging monitor, signalling to Rickets to stay put. He stood behind the technician, his hands held behind his back, looking over the rating's shoulder as he guessed an officer might. The screen showed blue as the technician scanned forward. He looked like he should be at school, Moss thought, instead of monitoring for potential enemies in the Southern Ocean. Moss flinched when the technician spoke, breaking the intense quiet of the scene.

"Horizon thermal imaging clear, sir," he said.

Lewis turned his head, saw Moss and ignored him, and said, "Scan thirty degrees relative, port and starboard."

"Scanning thirty degrees relative, port and starboard, aye, sir," the tech repeated.

He moved his fingers over the touch screen, and the blue on the monitor remained. Tapping the screen again, he scanned starboard. Blue filled the screen, except for a hint of yellow in the far corner.

"Faint reading at thirty degrees starboard, sir," he reported. "Imaging expanding to forty degrees."

The captain walked over to stand beside the technician as he increased the search area. Faint yellow marked the screen, a mere smudge of colour.

"Contact, sir!" the tech said.

"Remember your training," Lewis said. "Bearing and distance, please."

"Contact at bearing zero four four relative, distance twenty-two nautical miles, sir," he said.

"Bosun," Lewis said, "sound general stations. Let's get a recon drone there promptly."

Moss heard 'ayes' echoing from different parts of the bridge, followed by an alarm. A drone lifted from the deck and shot across the open sea in the direction of the contact. From where he stood, he searched for the monitor displaying the feed from the craft, and followed the captain over to it. Standing behind him, Moss watched the horizon from the camera of the drone. He squinted, trying to look for an object or ship at the line where water met sky, but the screen suddenly cut to static.

"Your monitor?" Lewis asked.

"No, sir," the technician answered. "Drone was disabled."

"Defensive screen, now," Lewis ordered. "Reduce speed to one third until we know what we're steaming into."

"Review your feed, please, Mr Simms," Lewis added to the tech.

Simms bent over his touch pad as two flocks of drones left the deck, one flying to port and the other to starboard. They took positions a kilometre away, matching the speed of the ship.

"There!" the technician reported.

Lewis bent over the tech's shoulder and viewed the screen, the image rewound to seconds prior to when it cut out. Simms slowed the feed and a white blur showed inside it just before the feed stopped.

"Probable drone, sir," Simms said.

"Probable?" Lewis asked.

Simms studied the blur again. "Definite, sir."

Lewis straightened up and walked to his chair in the centre of the bridge. "We have an unwelcome guest with probable hostile intent," he announced. "Let's send them a message to desist, Mr Aguirre."

"Send a message, aye, sir," he said. A missile shot away from the ship. "Message sent, sir."

"Incoming skimmer, sir," a rating at the radar reported. "Bearing zero four eight relative." Lewis turned and Moss followed his gaze. A flash of light in that direction signalled the end of the skimmer, as well as the drones self-destructing into it. Another flock lifted off the deck to take their place.

"Incoming drones, sir," the radar reported. "Bearing zero four eight relative. Too many to quantify on screen. ETA two minutes."

"Meet them," Lewis ordered. A flock of twenty drones rose from the deck and flew forward, spreading out into an open arc as they increased speed, the outside of the line bending forward towards the intruders.

"Helm, ten degrees starboard," Lewis said. "Let's get them where we want them."

The ship altered course and the incoming drones followed. "Send out our own birds, two flocks. It's time send a stronger message," Lewis added.

Sparks of light peppered the sky as drone met drone. Three managed to get through the screen and sped toward the corvette, only to spiral lifelessly as ship-based Pulsers disabled them. Immediately after the sky cleared, a new flock of drones took off, followed by another. Moss turned away from the window and moved closer to their operators stations. A split screen showed both a visual and a schematic of white dots against a blue screen. The Wainui sat at the bottom while their target lay towards the top right. The dots quickly closed the distance. Some disappeared, but most continued. Closer to their target, still more white lights went out. A black vessel appeared on the visual, vibrating as the drone sending the feed battled with strong winds. It grew closer, until nothing but black filled the screen, and finally static. The operator shifted the feed to another drone to see a black hull, followed by a glimpse of the deck, and then static once more.

"Multiple hits on target vessel, sir," he reported.

"Multiple strikes, sir," the operator of the second flock reported.

"Vessel is increasing speed, sir," the radar operator said. "Bearing a relative course of zero seven zero. Away from us, sir. She's starting to run."

"Akaroa is joining the fight, sir," the radio operator reported. "She's pursuing two contacts to the north west."

"Very well," Lewis said towards the radio. "Tell them 'good hunting'."

"Good hunting, aye," the operator repeated.

"Ready missiles," Lewis added. "Pepper them with another wave first."

Another collection of drones rose. Moss clenched and unclenched his hands, forcing himself to stand still.

"Second wave reaching target," the operator finally reported. "Multiple strikes."

"Vessel slowing, sir," the radar said. "Looks like they may have lost their engines."

"Very well," Lewis said. "Missile battery, time to sink our unwelcome guest."

"No!" Rickets shouted. "You can't do that!"

He moved towards the captain, his boot clunking on the deck. An officer nearby grabbed Rickets by the sleeve. He pulled his arm, trying to free himself as another clutched his other arm.

"Most of the men on that ship don't even know where they are," Rickets said. "They're practically slaves or prisoners."

"Get this man off the bridge," Lewis said.

"It's murder," Rickets protested as he was dragged to the door. "They don't even know where they are!" The closing door silenced his protest.

Lewis glared at Moss, who opened his hands. Lewis turned away towards the windows.

"He's right," Moss said. "Most of the crew on the boat are virtual prisoners."

Lewis stared forward before giving the command. "Aim for the bow," he ordered. "Above the waterline," he added. "Make sure they don't move any farther, send a cease-and-desist order and inform them of an imminent boarding. We'll expect no resistance and total cooperation. Make that clear, if they want to stay afloat. Let's go see what we've caught."

He continued to look out the windows as the first missile flew away from the ship. Moss made his way to the exit, his capital spent.

17

The vessel listed to its port and Naval attack drones hovered around it. Smoke still escaped from a recent fire in the stern where drones had targeted the engine room. A large section of the bow was nothing more than torn iron. The bow crane bent over the side, hanging onto the deck by a few stubborn bolts. Deck hands stood mutely as the *Wainui* drew alongside. Three men emerged from the wheelhouse, descended a flight of stairs to the forecastle deck, and stood waiting, each of their faces set in firm defiance. Lewis stepped onto the flight deck of the *Wainui* and lifted a loud speaker.

"This is Lieutenant Commander Jeremy Lewis of the Royal New Zealand Navy," he announced. "You are guilty of trespassing into the Exclusive Economic Zone of New Zealand, and firing upon a New Zealand warship. You will display any and all weapons in preparation for their surrender. All personnel will make themselves visible, and take a seated position on the deck. Prepare to be boarded."

He attached a translating app to the loud speaker and the instructions were repeated in Thai. One of the men on the forecastle spat on the deck before resuming his scowl. Lewis raised the loudspeaker again.

"I will give you to the count of ten to comply," he said, forcing restraint into each word. "Before you are fired upon."

He pointed at the hovering drones and a mounted fifty calibre machine gun before translating. The gun swivelled to point directly at the men on the forecastle. He raised his free hand, made a fist before showing one finger, then another, and then a third. Three men descended a flight of stairs to the trawl deck and stood with the deck hands.

"All crew," Lewis barked in the loud speaker. "Deck and factory."

A deckhand rose, shouted into a hatchway and more men came up to the deck. They sat behind the deckhands. The three men continued standing until Lewis turned and spoke to the seaman manning the mounting gun. It moved to point at the three, and they sat. Seamen hung fenders on the side of the *Wainui*, and grappling hooks fired across the short distance, latching onto the railing of the fishing vessel. Winches brought it closer until the inflatable fenders, that acted as buffers between the vessels, were pressed tight. Both ships rose and fell in the swell as one. Armed seamen from the *Wainui* leapt over the rails and pointed their weapons at the assembled men, while others searched below deck as well as the wheelhouse. Lewis glanced behind at Moss, who had managed to insert himself as a shadow into the scene.

"You're welcome to observe," he said. "But only that. Keep your mouth closed, until told otherwise."

He turned and stepped over onto the fishing boat before Moss could agree to the terms. He followed, accompanied by more armed seamen. Pieces of drone were mixed with scraps of metal from the deck and the dried remnants of a previous haul. The yoyo boom, used to help haul up the net, was missing, sheared off at its base. The gantry that spanned the deck was buckled in the middle, with its railing torn away. Lewis and Moss stepped carefully around the debris to where the men sat. The deck smelled of burnt diesel and dead fish. Lewis stood in front of the crew.

"The captain of this vessel," he said. "Identify yourself."

A translation followed from the device he held. Two men stood.

"I demand the use of your communications," one said in carefully articulated English.

"Your demands are immaterial," Lewis answered.

"My name is Chen Liu of the People's Liberation Navy," he persisted. "Sub-lieutenant Liu of the—"

"I don't give a good goddamned fuck who you are," Lewis said. "Ensign," he called. An officer stepped over and stood beside Lewis.

"Escort these two gentlemen to the brig," he said to the ensign. "And if they protest in any way, silence them," he added, looking at Liu.

Lewis approached the crew sitting on the deck and spoke to the translator. He held it up for all in front to hear.

"Will all deckhands please move towards the bow and take a seat," the device said.

The men in front looked at each other, and Lewis made a point of letting them see him look at the armed sailors around him. One got up and moved towards the bow, and the others followed.

"Now, Mr Cignet," Lewis said without turning, "is your opportunity to speak with these men." He reached back and handed Moss his phone with the translating device.

Moss swallowed. He tried to remember any training he may have had with a situation such as this, but drew a blank. He cleared his throat and looked at the men sitting in front of him. They looked at the deckhands sitting farther along the deck.

"My name is Michael Cignet," Moss started. "I am not in the Navy. I am an independent observer for the New Zealand Ministry of Fisheries."

Lewis stepped away a couple of metres when he heard the speech, creating distance between official and neutral. Moss held Lewis's phone towards them and listened as it repeated what he said in Thai. He took note of which crew looked towards him as they heard it. He squatted on the deck near one.

"Are you all Thai?" he asked, hearing it repeated in another language. "I can use this to translate to other languages."

He waited a moment, trying to make eye contact with those looking his way. "Khmer?" he asked. "Vietnam?" He continued to search their faces. "Myanmar?"

A thin man in the back faintly said, "Burmese."

Another said, "Khmer."

Moss set the translator. "We want you to know that we do not hold you responsible for the actions of your officers," he said, hearing it repeated three times. "They have broken both New Zealand and International Maritime Law, and they will be prosecuted for their crimes."

"If you have been mistreated in any way, or fear mistreatment, we can offer protection," Moss said, after the men processed that information. "If you feel unsafe on this vessel, you can board the *Wainui*, where you will be offered refuge." He listened to what he said again, and looked at Lewis when it had finished. Lewis nodded.

"It is difficult work out here," Moss said. "Is anyone on the ship injured? There is a ship's doctor on the *Wainui*. Does anyone require medical attention?"

Moss waited again for the translations, as well as any take-up time the men needed. A man near the back of the group stood and walked forward. He held out his arm for Moss to see; an infected cut ran from the base of his thumb to past his wrist. The edges of the wound were bright red, and the hand swollen. Another came forward, his skin covered in rash.

"See that Dr Roberts tends to these men," Lewis told a rating.

The seaman shouldered his weapon and guided the two to the railing. As they began to climb over, one of the men with the deckhands stood and shouted in Thai. Moss recognised him as the third man on the forecastle deck. Lewis took his phone from Moss, walked over and spoke softly, holding the translator for the man to hear. The man sat back down, and Lewis returned the device to Moss.

"Sometimes the factory can be a hard place to work," Moss said four times. "When is the last time your manager has beaten you?"

"He always uses the stick," one said. Moss lifted the phone to his ear and nodded.

"Nobody should work where they are beaten," Moss agreed. "In New Zealand there are laws prohibiting such treatment. You are in New Zealand now, and protected by her laws." He held the device towards them as the translations repeated his words.

"If you do not wish to continue to work under these conditions, the *Wainui* will transport you to New Zealand where you will be repatriated to your home country, or any claims for refugee status in New Zealand will be heard." Moss glanced at Lewis, who looked back with an expression between annoyance and impatience. As Lewis noticed the men squatting on the deck watching him, he smiled and nodded. Stepping over to Moss, he reclaimed his device.

"Any crew wishing sanctuary on the *Wainui* should stand now and follow Mr Cignet," he said. At the first translation, four men stood. Once the other two languages conveyed the message, eight more joined them.

"Mr Cignet, if you please," Lewis said.

Moss gestured to the men and crossed the deck. Seeing their crewmates leave, three more hurried and joined them. A rating passed Moss going the other way and spoke to Captain Lewis. Lewis nodded before issuing an order to an ensign and returning to the *Wainui* himself. Moss shepherded the crewmen with him towards a waiting rating before following Lewis to the bridge. Lewis went straight to a waiting phone and listened for a long time before speaking. When he finally did, it was brief.

"You've got to be kidding?" he said, before listening again.

"This is outrageous," he added, before listening more.

"Lieutenant Wise," he said, after returning the phone to its cradle. The officer approached, standing still beside his captain. "Please bring Sub-lieutenant Liu to the bridge."

Lewis stepped back from the phone with his hands clasped behind his back and jaw set. Liu entered the bridge with Wise, stepping confidently towards Lewis, who merely gestured to the phone. Liu lifted the receiver and listened, acknowledging from time to time in Mandarin.

"Lieutenant Wise," Lewis said. "Will you please escort Sub-lieutenant Liu of the People's Liberation Navy, and the captain of this ... fishing vessel, back to their own ship, please?"

"Sir," Wise answered.

"If you will," he said to Liu, indicating to the door.

Liu remained where he was. "You have my crew members on board," Liu said. "I demand they be released and returned to their vessel immediately."

Lewis faced Liu for the first time since he entered bridge, then glanced at Moss and smiled. "I have been ordered, Sub-lieutenant Liu," he said, "to see you off my ship. If you do not leave now, I will happily have you thrown over the side and consider my duty fulfilled."

Seconds ticked by as Liu stared back at Lewis, before he curtly turned on a heel and followed Lieutenant Wise from the bridge. Crew from the *Wainui* crossed back to their ship, released the grapnels, and let the fishing vessel drift away with its captain and Liu back on board.

Rickets lay on his bunk, his arms behind his head. Moss sat in the cabin's one chair, his feet propped against the bed.

"Should have kept my mouth shut," Rickets said. "Should have listened."

"Not at all, man." Moss said. "Best time to lose it, was when you lost it."

Rickets grinned. "Confined to quarters," he said. "Fucking typical."

"You earned it, buddy," Moss said.

"You're sure none of them knew a factory hand named Tom?" Rickets asked.

"Nah, wrong ship, I'm afraid."

"And the others down here?"

"The *Akaroa* was ordered to desist her attack and return to the Aucklands, same as us," Moss said.

"Anything to do with the Chinese officer we caught, do you think?"

"You like asking dumb questions, don't you, Rickets?" Moss asked. "The Prime Minister is in Beijing re-negotiating the free-trade agreement for the umpteenth time, and we go and arrest a Chinese naval officer on a goddammed ghost ship deep in our *Eazy*. They're probably talking about you at cabinet level."

"Nice thought," Rickets said. "Shitty deal, though. Fucker sails away free."

"Gets towed away, free," Moss corrected. "And if it wasn't for you, that ship and its naval officer would be at the bottom of the sea, as well as all hands, deck and factory, and we'd be back at the squid grounds."

The smile on Rickets' face grew into a satisfied grin. "True that, bro," he said.

18

Mel answered the door to see a large PAC-Man standing in the corridor. She smiled.

"You must be Patrick," she said. "Come in!"

"Call me Rickets," he said, stepping into the apartment. "Even my own mother doesn't call me Patrick."

"Moss, your friend is here," she called to the other room. "Come here," she said to Rickets, opening her arms. "It is so great to finally meet you."

He shifted a large box under an arm and bent over to hug her.

"How did somebody so short end up with such a tall bean pole as Moss?" he asked.

"Persistence," she answered. "And lots of flowers."

He handed her the box. "A little gift from the company store," he said.

"Yummy," she said. "Hoki fillets," she read, "*Caught Wild in New Zealand*. I'll buy another freezer to put this in. It's huge!"

"And she's a hard-core vegetarian, Rickets," Moss said. He wrapped his arms around Rickets, both competing in squeezing the air out of the other.

"It's good to see you," Moss said. "Come in, don't just stand there."

"Hey, I was busy offending your lady with fish," he said. "And it's great to finally meet you, Mel. This guy never stopped talking about you."

"I'll bet," Mel said. She set the box of fish on the kitchen bench.

"Drink?" Moss asked. "I'm afraid it's nothing but girlie beer in this house."

"As long as you're buying, mate," Rickets said, taking a bottle. "Colourful label. Usually a bad sign."

"From a new brewery nearby," Moss said. "Seems to be a new one opening every other week, and it wouldn't do to not at least taste them."

"If you say so," Rickets said.

"Sit down, you two," Mel said. "We went all-out on dinner tonight," she added once they sank into the sofas. "Pizza should get here in about twenty."

"Perfect," Rickets said. "Meat supreme?"

"Funny guy," Mel said.

"How long are you in town?" Moss asked.

"Ship out in two days for the Chatham Rise. Six-week trip," he answered. "Then another. Back-to-back before a stint off."

"I'm surprised you want to still to fish," Mel said.

"It gets under your skin," Rickets said. "And I like it. As well as the pay cheque. I'm saving for a house, and while I'm at sea, I can't spend any of it."

"But where people can shoot at you," Mel said.

"Yeah, nah," Rickets said. "Things have calmed down a lot since the fisheries deal. If the Chinese are getting a twenty percent share of our quota, they're not going to be sending their pirates in to fuck with, sorry, I mean mess with, the deal. Good old-fashioned gangsta shake down, protecting us from their own ghosts. They'll carry observers, at least that's part of the deal."

"Who will each be monitored by a Chinese observer. I can't imagine trying to work with somebody looking over your shoulder," Moss said.

"Says the guy whose job was to watch others work," Rickets said.

"Not the same," Moss protested.

"Yeah, I hear you," Rickets said. "If it keeps being as quiet as it is out there, I'll probably end up back in the factory. Then I'll think about getting out."

"Says the fisherman who doesn't like to work with fish," Moss said. "But I think you're wrong there. There's going to be others sneaking in. Especially after we backed down and cut a deal."

"Where is your house going to be, Rickets?" Mel asked, steering the conversation towards land.

"I don't know," he said. "I like Nelson, but I miss home."

"Where is that?"

"East Coast. Gizzy," Rickets said. "Or twenty kilometres north, in a little slice of paradise called Whangara. Traditional land rights there, no First-Time lottery and all that."

"Nice. Surfing and horse riding?" Moss asked.

"To your heart's content."

Mel rose to get the door when the bell rang, swiped for the pizzas and brought them to the coffee table. She opened the lids and the smell of melted cheese and pepperoni filled the room.

"I thought you might like this," she said, offering him a plate. She put a slice of vegetarian on her own.

"Keep hold of this one," Rickets told Moss.

"No argument there," Moss said, wavering between pizzas before taking a piece from each.

"Tell me," he said between bites. "What have you heard about Anna and Toby?"

"Rumour has it the company gave Anna a rather substantial pay-out to stay out of court," Rickets said. "Loos put them in a rather untenable position. It's all hush-hush and sealed with a confidentiality clause, though. But I know how substantial it was, because she told me. She doesn't have to sail again, not that she would. In fact, she'd like to live as far away from the water as possible. She even me asked me what Taihape was like. Saw it on the map, smack dab in the middle of the North Island. Taihape," he said again, shaking his head.

"How is she doing?"

"Okay, I think," Rickets said. "She'll need time to heal, if that's possible. But I think she's going to be all right."

"And Toby?"

"And Toby," Rickets confirmed. "He's on the mend slowly, but he'll get right. Still has a little droop," Rickets added, pulling at his face with a finger. "But it seems our Mr Cooper has been offered the First Mate position on the *Swarbrick*. The old First moved over to captain the *Ardern*."

"Well, well," Moss said. "Is he going to take it?"

"I get the impression Anna would rather he stay shore-side, but it's too good to pass up, and she knows that too," Rickets said. "Company told him to take his time deciding, that it's on hold with his name on it."

"Nice," Moss said.

"How about you?" Rickets asked. "What have you been up to?"

"Oh, looking for work," Moss said. "Trying to find that niche just right for my skill set."

"Skill set," Rickets grinned, "watching others work."

"He's been canvassing with his resumé, if that's the right way to put it," Mel said. "But something will come up."

"True," Rickets said, sitting forward. "But maybe you're looking in the wrong places."

"Meaning?"

"The company would hire you, no doubt about it," Rickets said.

"He's just come home," Mel said. "His girlfriend would be very upset if he went off fishing."

"Not fishing," Rickets said. "In the office. They need people who understand the quota, and understand the government. Besides, you're a hero over there. You saved three of their people. You've got what I believe is called *capital*. I'm surprised you haven't hit them up yet, cashed it in." He took another slice of pizza and tilted his empty bottle at Moss.

Moss got up to fetch more bottles, brought them to the table and opened one for Rickets.

"And, you've got people on the inside to talk you up," Rickets continued. He took a swig, swallowed. "Your lady is smiling at me," he said.

"I think you just gave me something to smile about," she said. She reached over and took Moss's hand.

"I might just do that," Moss said. "I've always thought of the industry as the other side. Maybe it's time to switch." He slid down in his seat until he was reclining more than sitting. He stretched his feet out past the coffee table and crossed his legs at the ankles. He smiled, scratched the new scar on his head, and nodded.

"Yeah," he said. "I might just do that."

Rickets watched Moss recline before leaning towards Mel. "But tell me. This has been perplexing me for some time," he said.

"What is it?" she said.

"How did this guy ever get the name Moss? I mean, who would even want to be called that?"

"Seriously?" she asked. "To be honest, he's never told me. I like to think it's because he just kind of grows on you. But, have you ever seen him try to grow a beard?"

Rickets shook his head. "Nothing aside from a few days stubble."

She raised a finger to her face and let it hop from place to place. "It grows in odd patches," she said, "and it looks surprisingly like something you'd see growing on a tree."

END

ACKNOWLEDGEMENTS

Pirates Come Down was mainly written during down time while I was at sea, and I would like to thank the vessels and crew on which I observed. I am not allowed to say what ships, or what crew, but I hope you know that I am grateful for your support and advice. This includes the galley hand who taught me how to swear in Thai, officers who told me the various parts of the machinery and answered my 'what if' questions, and the many crew on the deck and factory who were just being themselves.

Many resources were utilised in researching this story, but I would like to single out, and recommend, two books for those interested in deep sea fishing, as well as the subantarctic islands. *The Outlaw Ocean: Crime and Survival in the Last Untamed Frontier,* by Ian Urbina, is "Just incredible." Those are the words used by Naomi Klein to describe the work, and I wholeheartedly agree with her. Urbina describes a reality on the high seas that more need to know about. Please read it. Know where your food comes from. I have heard the author on the radio talking about his work around the globe, and it makes me glad that New Zealand is where it is, and that it takes the management of its waters, and the wellbeing of those working on it, very seriously.

Regarding the Auckland Islands, *The Island of the Lost: Shipwrecked at the Edge of the World,* by Joan Druett, is a fascinating portrayal of the wreck of the *Grafton* and the struggle of the five men aboard in surviving over sixteen months on the largest island of the group, Auckland Island. All five survived the ordeal. Shortly after their stranding, and unbeknownst to them, another ship, the *Invercauld*, ran aground off the north west of Auckland Island. Of the twenty-two crew, only three lived. It is not only a story of shipwreck, but of leadership and camaraderie, of the best, and the less than best, of human nature. One result of these wrecks was the establishment of castaway depots in various locations of the subantarctic islands. If you're planning (or not) to be stranded there, the depot in this book (found by Rickets, Anna and Toby) on Deep Inlet is purely fictitious.

Finally, I would like to thank my friends and critics Andrew McKenna, Tony Armstrong, Eddie Nolan and Susie Lee for their reader's eye and encouragement, and the editorial pen of Siobhan Haley at the Writer's Apothecary.

Bonus Reading

FROM: JOURNEY TO THE STARS

Short stories inspired by the deep-sea fisheries. From the collection by the author:

Eighteen science and climate fiction stories from the bottom of the ocean to the depths of space.

Available now from online book retailers.

Benthic Material

As the narrator describes, benthic material is found on the ocean floor. In this story, he tells some trainees what got hauled up ...

"Weirdest thing I ever caught?"

Of course, they would ask that. They just spent a whole day on non-quota by-catch. Corals, sponges, plants, molluscs, wood, rocks. Anything that the net of a bottom trawler hauls up with its catch has to be recorded. Bottom trawling can be very harmful to the sea floor, so all the pictures and notes they'll be taking are a part of trying to mitigate that.

Stories abound. One of the most popular involves a washing machine. It's illegal to dump any rubbish into the ocean, so the fishing boat had to take the rusty, scum encrusted thing with them and land it with the rest of their catch.

"It's okay," the government fishery observer told the skipper. "It won't count as part of your quota." Funny guy, if it ever, really, happened.

"That will cost you another pint," I answered.

They burst out laughing as a trainee arrived at that exact moment with a tray full of pints. He placed one in front of me, a tall guy who said his name was Mike, but everybody called

Tree. Now I was stuck. I nodded my thanks to Tree, picked up the pint and took a sip. I lost count of the drinks. The empties were cleared away far too fast in this pub. Three? Four? Sailors are known for having a terrible relationship with alcohol. They are dry for weeks while at sea, but get mind-shatteringly wasted when on land. I wasn't one of those. At least, I didn't want to be. I was merely visiting here, down for a day to cover some material on their course. This was almost like a holiday, of sorts, so a few drinks couldn't hurt.

They were a good cohort. They got on well together and took in most of what was delivered. And, as they hadn't been to sea yet, they were hungry for anything an experienced observer had to tell them. They'll learn most of the job on their first trip, going out with another observer and shadowing them for weeks. Most of what we teach them on land is just the government covering its ass. Observers are their most 'at risk' employees. They board a fishing vessel and go hundreds of kilometres off shore, watching and recording what is caught, ensuring the company keeps to their limit, testing the health of the fish caught. And recording anything that isn't a fish that happens to wind up in the net.

"Weirdest thing! Come on!" the loud, young one named Zac called.

He's going to have to rein it in on board if he wants to have a good time, but he seems quite socially astute. He can read what is appropriate, what isn't, and when. I'm sure he'll be fine. I take another drink and wait for the chatter at the end of the table to die out. The beer in this town tastes too good. I have definitely had too much.

"Weirdest thing I ever caught," I repeated for dramatic effect. "You know, I didn't catch anything. I was just there to observe others catching—"

"Come on! You know what we mean!" Zac said.

So, I told them. It was my sixth or seventh trip out. I was getting into the groove of the lifestyle. Six or eight weeks out, then as long ashore as I wanted, with a fat pay cheque waiting. The first year I chased those pay days, and kept signing up for another trip a week or two after returning. Every international ship was required, by law, to have an observer on board, and most national ones in vulnerable fisheries did too, so there was never a shortage of work. I sailed on the Russian ships, eating at the captain's table. I sailed on the Korean, with their Indonesian crews. We got a three-hundred-dollar budget on those for 'stores', which meant comfort food that Russians or Koreans just don't have. Part of being 'at risk' is being looked after, so a usually tight-fisted Ministry was generous for a change.

It was on a Korean vessel. I can't remember the name, and couldn't tell you anyway. Confidentiality and all that. You have to learn to be careful about talking about your job. What ship you're on, where they fished, what you thought about them. You have to keep it to yourself.

The trainees are all given an article that appeared in the Herald. A reporter rode along with a Russian fishing vessel, and not being able to speak the language turned to the one Kiwi on board, the fisheries observer. The result was a very interesting article, and an observer promptly losing their job. Sounds harsh, but we're talking about commercially sensitive practices, and a relationship between industry and government built on trust. You don't talk to the press unless cleared. You don't mess with that trust.

I didn't know if I would like the Korean boats. The factories below decks have lower ceilings, so there is no grate between your gum boots and the water sloshing over the deck. They eat different foods. They adhere to a hierarchy. On a Kiwi boat you might eat anywhere in the mess. On a Korean boat, you're considered a junior officer and must dress and act like it. That means eating at the captain's table. The Indonesian-only crew eat after the Korean officers, and you, are finished.

I actually liked their order. And I may be soft, but the food on the captain's table was better than what the crew ate. The only thing I spent a chunk of those three hundred dollars on was fresh ground coffee. My cabin reeked of it. It wasn't that bad at all—except for the swaying back and forth, the occasional bout of sea sickness, and the ever-present smell of fish.

It was a big haul. The fishing master had set the net at a beautiful location. The net surfaced and my first 'eyeball estimate' was that it was a lot. I was going to have my work cut out for me on this one. I made sure I had my camera, my notepad, and pencils to spare. The winches slowly dragged the net on board and I could see they had hit a motherload of orange roughy. But there was bound to be a large by-catch impact. As the net continued to be brought aboard, I noticed a large bulge in the middle. For all I knew, it could have been a washing machine, or a protected species like a basking shark, so I waited as the net was lifted and emptied into the pound, the stainless-steel tanks that hold the catch until it's processed in the factory below.

Only the bulge didn't shift. Fish streamed around it, but it stayed where it was. When the net was empty, the bulge moved, as if something was struggling inside it. Because something was struggling inside it. The bulge moved towards the mouth of the net, which was just above the pound. The Indonesian deckhands backed away. I backed away. We watched as the bulge made its way to the mouth, and then stepped out of the net.

It's hard to describe what it was. I feel like something has scratched away at the picture in my mind, because that's probably what happened. It was about a metre and a half tall, standing on legs, with arms moving angrily beside it. I use the terms legs and arms and angry because they seem to fit, not because they're accurate. It had a head, of sorts, and a mouth, or at least a breathing hole, that sucked in air in wet gasps. It had eyes, I'm sure of that. It turned its head and scanned the deck and all of us standing on it. I don't think calling it an 'it' is appropriate, but I don't know what else to use. It was definitely a something, but I don't know what. Its eyes met mine and I literally staggered back a step.

Then it spoke. I mean, it made sounds out of what might have been a mouth. I jumped when it did. The Indonesian deck hands jumped as well, so I know they heard it, whatever they said after. And I know they understood what it was saying, same as me.

It was clear it wasn't happy.

"What the fuck are you assholes doing!"

I stood there, mouth open, totally frozen on the spot. I heard shouting in Indonesian, heard a crash as, I assumed, a deck hand or two were stumbling backward and falling over, trying to get as far from what they had caught as possible. I should have been doing the same, but like I said, I just couldn't move. It took a step towards me, waving what I think was an arm.

"I come to this speck of a planet to visit the only really sentient type of life it has, and you dumb fucks run a rake through it!"

If it wanted an answer, I couldn't give it. I think I even wet myself. It took another step towards me and pointed at my chest as if it were a target.

"You! Dumb! Fucks!" The words sounded like distant thunder, a growing rumble that promised so much more.

Then it spread its arms, or whatever they were, as wide as they could go. I don't know how, some sort of intuition, but I had an idea of what it was going to do with those arms. So, I did all I could do. I fell to the deck, assumed the foetal position, closed my eyes as tight as I could, and put my hands over my ears.

I can only guess that it clapped its hands together because I didn't see. The deck shook, and even with my eyes closed,

I felt blinded by a flash of light. I felt myself slide backward across the trawl deck until I hit the rail. I stayed curled up right there for I don't know how long, until a deck hand eventually shook me by the shoulder. He shook for quite a while. I finally opened my eyes to see all of the Indonesians standing over and looking down at me. One, the only one that knew some English, bent a knee and felt my head.

"You okay?" he asked.

I jerked away from him, trying to scramble farther away from the net, but I was already as far I could get without running through a hatch. My eyes must have been the size of saucers as I looked up and down the deck.

It was empty.

"Where is it? Where is it?" I kept asking, and the deck hand's face looked more and more worried.

"Where is what?" he asked.

I must have continued asking the same question, because he stopped trying to reach me. I remember being lifted off the deck, carried through the passage and into my quarters. I remember the Korean mate, who was also the ship's medic, sliding a needle into me. Then I don't remember anything for quite a while.

When I woke up, it seemed that the crew didn't remember anything either, just that the observer seemed to have some sort of breakdown on deck during a haul. My talking about the by-catch only seemed to reinforce that. They put up with me for the rest of trip, but I've never been given a Korean ship since.

My pint was empty, but nobody got up to refill it. They all sat there, staring, waiting for more, waiting for an explanation or something, some sort of resolution, or at least a punch line. But there wasn't any.

The Irish one, Rachel, looked at me with a particularly Irish smirk. I'm sure she thought I just described a leprechaun and am probably making fun of her. She doesn't think it's true, what I saw.

A Little Night Action

They think. They feel. They want to live, just like us. Using the latest technology, activists (or, some might argue, terrorists) fight for animals that aren't able to defend themselves ...

She lifted the hard plastic case out of the locker and set it on the table. Releasing the clips and opening the lid, she gazed at the contents.

"Where's David?" she asked without turning.

"He's still sick."

"How can somebody be sick for three days?" She grabbed the table as the boat swayed, leaned over to view down the hatch and saw David lying on a bench.

"Hey!" she shouted. "Are you in this or not?"

David turned a pale face and looked at her with glassy eyes. He slowly closed them and lay his head back down.

"Fuck!" she said. "Get over here, kid, you're David now."

The young man left the railing he was clutching and staggered to the table in the centre of the deck. He looked at her, waiting for instructions. He didn't know how to be David. David had recruited him for the trip, but he hardly knew David. It was his first action, so when asked to come, he accepted without having to think twice. New recruits could wait months, or more, before they were trusted to go out. As he watched her marvel at what was in the case, he realised he didn't even know her name. She turned it so he could see inside.

"Come closer," she said. "Touch it."

He wrinkled his nose.

"This is what it's all about, kid. It'll be a game changer." She spoke loudly and passionately in that way that both frightened and reassured him. "They'll think twice before sucking everything out of the ocean."

She looked at him, waiting for him to reach out. He hesitated.

"Oh, for fuck's sake," she said. "Can you smell anything? No? That means it's fresh." She laughed at a joke he didn't understand.

He reached out a finger and touched it, pressing against its flesh. He ran it down its side. Then he lifted his finger to his nose and smelled it.

"You're such a moron," she said.

"The scales look so real."

"The whole thing looks real," she said. "Watch this." She tapped a key on her laptop and an image filled the screen. The cabin came into focus, and in front of that, themselves.

"That's us!" he said. He turned and looked at the case, and then to the screen to see the back of his head.

"Perfect optics. That's how we find the net," she said. "Then the equivalent of a brick of C-4 ends their fucking fishing."

"That has what in it? You made me touch it!"

"Relax, newbie," she said. She squinted her eyes as she grinned. "It isn't activated yet. I'll do that when it's in their net. They won't know what hit them. They might cotton on after three or four ships catch our babies."

"I don't want to kill fish," he said. "I'm here to protect them."

"Is this your first time out?" she asked.

"Yeah, David said—"

"Fuck me," she interrupted. "Listen. The fish in the net, they're already dead. They've been suffocated and crushed to death. It's bloody horrible. But you have to step up now that Sicko is incapacitated. Consider it a battlefield promotion. We're here to stop the slaughter of thousands, of millions. Are you going to flake out now?"

"No," he said. "I want to stop it too."

"Good, so get ready."

She left him by the case and walked through the cabin to reach the wheelhouse. She studied the screens illuminating the room, making little sense of what she saw.

"How we doing, skipper?"

"Almost in range," he said.

"Great. That them there?" she asked, pointing out the window at red and white lights rising and falling across the black water.

"That's them," the skipper said. "Red over white, fishing tonight. That's what those lights mean. Fuckers work around the clock, never give it a rest."

"Will they see us?"

"Yep. But I hacked the automatic identification system. According to their radar we're a charter out for a bit of night fishing," he said. "If you're going to do this, now's the time. I'll keep us local."

She returned to the case. The young man stood beside it just as she had left him, not sure what to do with his hands or the rest of his body. She shook her head and typed in the activation code on her laptop. The eyes inside the case lit red. Waving the young man over, she indicated for him to pick it up. He took it in both hands, bumping the table with his hip as the swell lifted the boat.

"Watch it, for fuck's sake," she hissed. "Now put it in the harness."

He followed her finger to a length of line tied to straps made of rubber, carried it over and carefully inserted it. Now that it was out of the case, he could see it was mechanical. Its body was narrow and silver, with a dorsal fin rising out of its back, and the tell-tell dark markings on its rounded head just like a silver warehou. But its red, illuminated eyes and jointed tail were definitely not natural.

She bent over her laptop. "Now lower it over," she said, but he didn't hear.

He waited, watching her. For somebody so small, she exuded a great deal of strength, he thought. If she weren't so scary, he might have been attracted to her.

"New David!" she called. Not hearing a response, she turned and faced him. "Okay, so what is your name, then?'

"Cody," he said.

"Of course it is," she said. "Cody, raise the antenna in the dorsal fin and lower the goddamned fish over the side. And be careful!"

He noticed the small wire in the fin, pinched it and pulled. It withdrew from the fish for thirty centimetres before stopping. He raised the fish over the railing and reached out over the water as he lowered the harness. When it was fully submerged, the mechanical fish squirmed as if testing its muscles before darting out and disappearing into the dark sea. Cody joined her at the laptop, peering at the screen.

"It's dark," he said.

"Of course it is," she said. "It's under the water, and it's night time." She tapped a key and adjusted the fish's course. "Watch this," she added. "Thermal imaging."

She pressed another key and the dark on the screen turned a hazy navy blue. After several minutes a yellow and orange glow appeared. She guided the fish over the top of the mass before taking it around the other side.

"Butchers!" she spat. "Look at all of them."

She guided the fish back over the haul until reaching the gaping mouth of the trawl net. Turning it around, she let it be swallowed. The yellow and orange glow grew larger until it surrounded the fish. She typed commands on the laptop and it squirmed itself deep into the mass of the dead and dying.

Tears ran down her cheeks. "So many," she said. "So many ..."

Cody watched her as she stood in front of the screen, not knowing what to do or say, gingerly holding himself away, as if she had the equivalent of a brick of C-4 hidden somewhere inside her.

"What do we do now?" he asked carefully.

"Wait," she said, wiping her eyes with the back of her hand, sniffing, and wiping snot away with her palm. "We wait until they haul."

They stood over the laptop as minutes turned into an hour. Finally, motion sensors on the fish showed it was rising. She switched the image to visual and the dark on the screen turned to dim light. Then the light increased and they saw all the fish around theirs, and the view tumbled as it fell into the waiting pound below, the tank holding the catch until it was beheaded, sliced, gutted, weighed and frozen with others into solid blocks to then be shipped around the world to be fried, grilled, broiled or barbequed, and finally eaten. She felt the blood rush to her cheeks as she thought about it. She typed a code into her laptop, and stood up straight. Her eyes were now dry and her face set in a fierce frown as she pressed the tab key.

A large flash lit the night before the sound of the explosion reached them. They turned and watched the trawler burning across the water. The radio in the wheelhouse crackled.

"Mayday! Mayday! Mayday!" it screamed at them until the skipper turned the volume down. "Mayday! This is the fishing vessel *Armitage*. We are in need of immediate assistance. *Romeo! Romeo!* Please render assistance."

The three stared at the radio. David raised his head weakly and watched it with them. They flinched as it barked again.

"*Romeo! Romeo!* Please respond!" it called. "This is the fishing vessel, *Armitage*. We are in need of—" The skipper turned off the radio.

"Who's *Romeo?*" the woman asked.

"We are," the skipper said. "At least on their radar." He opened the throttle and the boat lurched forward and sped away from the scene.

"Nice," she said, grabbing hold of a bench to steady herself. "*Romeo*, oh *Romeo*, wherefore art thou, *Romeo?*"

TO LEARN MORE ABOUT CHRISTOPHER'S BOOKS, VISIT HIM AT:

www.christophermcmaster.com